LUV SLAPS

Luv Slaps

Stories

John Oliver Hodges

BROKEN TRIBE PRESS

CONTENTS

for

Jasmine

a woman

of healing

aigoos

GARY GETS GARY

WE HEARD THE SNIFFLES, the sniffling, the mumbling things to himself that we couldn't tell what it was he was mumbling. The mumbling went on for hours, so we stuffed towels under the closet door, thinking we'd mute the mumbling, something to where we didn't have to hear the mumbling, or the sniffling. But the mumbling and sniffling seeped under the door. The mumbling and sniffling seeped through the towels into our dreams. In the morning the mumbling was in the room again with us. And the sniffling. So we opened our eyes. She looked at me. She said, "We should call somebody."

I said, "Let's go in the closet."

We went in the closet where once we were in there the mumbling stopped. We pressed ears to the wall. All was quiet. If we heard it again, we said, we'd call some damn body.

I got a job in packing.

She got on as a waitress.

Our futon, when we'd first spread it over the floor, what a fat puffy magic cloud it was! Two weeks later our cloud was a knobby pancake, and whenever we did it I like turned into a sobbing infant baby below her. I was the gooey sobbing slobbering thing grabbing up all gobblingly at her breasts, clutching them and squeezing into them in the wet misery thinking *Mommy!* like some baby might think *Mommy! Oh Mommy, Mommy, Mommy!*

The mumbling and sniffling came weekends. Then we started hearing screams in the mumbling and sniffling.

We said we'd call somebody.

But Mondays rolled around and we took off into other things. We blotted out the screams. We plowed over the whole idea of screams with other, stupid, silly things. We bulldozed our screams with our deal, the ordeal. She would cry. That was my queue.

"What?"

"You know."

"I do?"

"Yes, why do you always have to be so mean?"

"I haven't said five words."

"When will I stop paying for this?"

I tried to comfort her, licking her tears. Sometimes it worked. Other times she wept harder. I didn't mind swallowing her tears, but tears, I think, carry emotional weight, and can upset your stomach and possibly make you depressed.

One day I saw the guy. I was leaving the complex when he came walking down the narrow hall under the dim spooky lights, his gut leading the way. Had a cap on. Carried a bouquet of red roses. We slid to the sides to let each other pass. As we slid, I said, "Oh, I see you have a date."

"A present for my son," the man said.

We turned and faced each other, and he put the roses in his left hand so that he could bring his right hand up for a shake. I shook it, saying to myself, *You're supposed to call somebody, not shake his hand!*

"I'm in the printing business," the man said, and said, "Can I ask you a question? Has Gary kept you up?"

"Gary?"

"Last neighbor told the landlord I was beating Gary up, but the divorce is very clear. I get Gary when I get Gary, Friday night to Sunday and on this day and that day. It's very clear what days I get Gary."

"Oh, I was wondering," I said.

"It's a medical condition. A disease. Today is Gary's birthday. I'm Gary, by the way."

"Hey, I'm Gary too."

"Trippy."

His teeth had rotten spots on them. He looked at my shoes. I could tell he didn't like that we had the same name. "Gary is a fighter," he said. "The previous neighbors were very cruel. Gary needs encouragement. He needs to feel treasured and celebrated even when it's not his birthday. He is very needy, you know what I mean?"

"Yeah, sure."

"What Gary doesn't need is a boot in the face, like what happened with these other neighbors, how they called the landlord. It really defies belief how a person could do a thing like that, but people are people. What can you do?"

"Yeah," I said.

"Anyway, I'll see you around," Gary said.

I continued down the hall. I opened the door to the outside and kicked myself in the head all the way to Big Star where I bought garlic because she forgot the garlic earlier when she went to Big Star for sauce ingredients.

Back at our place I mentioned bumping into Gary, and I told her what Gary said.

"Did you believe Gary?"

"Not exactly, but he did seem to believe himself."

"Well, why didn't you say something?"

"We've never actually heard him beating Gary up."

She started clapping hooray for the genius.

"You've had plenty of time to call," I said.

"I'm calling Monday. Government things are open nine to five, Monday through Friday."

"They have answering machines."

"How can you say that to me?"

"I'm sadistic, remember?"

"Yeah, and a fucking asshole's what you are."

It gets in you like you want to smash something. That's what she wanted. Me to lose it, go crazy. Then, once I made a fool of myself, I'd get to feel all guilty. Her birthday was in three days. She still felt shitty, lousy, dirty, that's why she cried so much on the trip down. In Chicago we'd had a time of it. Had it been up to me, a stranger would have come along and murdered me. The stranger could've blown my brains out, fine by me. The stranger could've strangled me. I was open to being stabbed. She needed cheering up. I knew I would get no credit for this, but I grabbed the dish strainer full of dishes. I slammed it onto the floor.

She went to cutting garlic with a vengeance, really gripping that knife, letting me have it over the kind of guy

I am. *Cowardly. Selfish. Unconscionable. Violent.* It was good we weren't married because then I'd be a wife beater. Did I want to be a wife beater?

"I didn't touch you."

"But you could have. You almost did. You wanted to so I don't even see what's the difference."

Getting ready for bed she still was at it, wordlessly, but at it, when the mumbling started, and then the screaming. It was pathetic, this crying screaming sobby sound that you couldn't even tell what it was that was being sobbed and screamed about. We dropped our thoughts, crawled into the closet, and heard Gary say, "I bring you roses!"

"I told you what I wanted!"

"Smell them, Gary!"

"I hate roses!"

We heard scuffling and the sobbing got louder and then it was only the screams.

I can't even think these things, but passionate rips were in her special flowery dress. In Chicago, where I threw the TV out the window. The guy the TV nearly landed on always walked around the neighborhood with a brass pyramid on his head. He said to funnel energy.

But the screams were loud that night. This was the sound of our new life. The kid didn't want roses. The screams came at intervals, as those that might be created with a belt, the putting on, the taking off of it upon a body. The engagement of such a process would surely create the sounds we heard.

ALIVE IN THE JUNGLE

A PHOTO OF BIRDIE as a much thinner woman graced the Browns' living room wall, she in jodhpurs and pith helmet standing with a rifle behind a bunch of dead animals. Some of Birdie's African game she had stuffed and shipped home to Florida. We're talking warthogs with snarling snouts and horns tusking out, a panther and many small pig type things I couldn't tell you the names of. At night moonlight flitted through the tall gatehouse windows, and the animal teeth shone white in the darkness.

I loved the old gatehouse, where after school I hung out with Butch. We would climb through a hole in his closet into the spacious area between the ceiling and roof, and smoke cigarettes as the pigeons there roosted and flapped. Sometimes we went out on the tin roof and latched onto an oak branch. We'd scrabble down the tree and run into the plantation field and wrestle. When we got tired, torn grass on our faces, we'd look around and imagine the old days, when the fancily dressed up gatehouse slaves let merchants onto the grounds in wagons hauling spices and wines. I loved spending the night with Butch, but Birdie's dead animals scared me, all but for the monkey that Birdie had shot out of a tree when she traveled the world. The monkey's name was Dave.

One day I took Dave into the bathroom, and sat on the toilet with him. I petted Dave. I said Dave's name. "Dave, I love you," I whispered in his ear. Would I be taking too much liberty to kiss Dave on his tiny nose? I wanted to, so did it real quick and Dave didn't mind. "Oh Dave," I said. "If you were my monkey I would smother you with kisses," and I said a bunch of other stuff to Dave.

"Hey, what're you doing in there?" somebody said, and knocked. It was Roy.

"Nothing, I'm almost done."

"Who are you in there with?"

"I'll be out in a minute."

"Are you taking a shit? Hurry up, I need to use it."

I tried lifting the bathroom window, thinking I would drop Dave down into the dirt then carry him back inside later, but Roy again said to hurry.

Roy was the oldest of Birdie's "white trash brood," as the neighborhood kids called the Browns. The Browns were bastards, they said, but when I left the bathroom Roy grabbed my shoulder. Dave's furry creature features flipped around from behind me, drawing Roy's attention. "What were you doing in there with my mother's monkey?" he wanted to know.

"Nothing."

"Were you talking to him?"

"I was looking at him," I said, and explained that my

dad always said it was better to do two things at once if possible. That's why there were political books and newspapers in our bathroom. When my dad was in there he read so as to not waste time, and time was life and life was precious.

Roy said, "Be careful with him. Already pieces have been falling out of his pecker. Put it back where it's supposed to be, and don't touch it again."

Roy went in the bathroom and I put Dave back on the mantle with his legs dangling over. "Don't worry, Dave," I whispered in his ear, and I whispered, "I love you, Dave. Don't ever forget that I love you," and I left the gatehouse and returned to my ranch house for dinner, and thought of Dave the whole time as I ate. I had always wanted a pet, but my dad would never allow it. He and my mom hated animals. Animals were dirty. You had to feed animals and take care of animals. The only thing animals were good for were taking bites out of. My mom made a killer meatloaf that we always ate with ketchup.

Days passed. I kept thinking about Dave. I started thinking I was weird for thinking about Dave, so tried hard to forget Dave. Then one night in bed I missed Dave so bad that my heart hurt. I pictured Dave swinging in the jungle through the trees and jumping and shrieking before Birdie shot him, knocking him out of his joyful noise and play. It made me cry, thinking about how unfair that was, and whenever I thought of stuff like this, I wished I could stay little forever. I hated growing. I wished I could be a monkey, alive in the jungle like Dave had once been.

I needed Dave. Within Dave's body was a voice that called out to me for help. So I rode by the gatehouse to get closer to Dave. In my gatehouse ride-bys I took note of when the Browns were gone. Finally I hid my bike in some bushes, and snuck in through the back door of the gatehouse. I went in the hall and grabbed Dave and ran with him to my bike, our hearts beating wild and afraid. I even kissed Dave as I ran. I couldn't wait to be alone with Dave.

I pulled my red bike out of the woods, and put Dave on the handlebars, holding his shoulder with one hand. It was a risky way to ride, but I made it past the gatehouse and turned into the greater part of Waverly Hills, where houses were of brick and solid with shiny paint, sturdy mailboxes and cut yards. The people I passed looked at me funny, but it was October, so this could be a Halloween thing. I was almost home. Soon Dave and I would begin our life together. I had just turned onto Lothian when there, walking along with his electric guitar, was Roy Brown, and right beside him was Butch.

Roy said, "What the fuck you doing with my mother's monkey, bitch?" and pushed me and Dave, bike and all, into the ditch. Dave flew and tumbled like a crinkly ball through the grass of somebody's yard. "I told you not to fuck with him," Roy said, and set his guitar down as Butch, who was my age, pinned me to the ground. I pushed Butch off, as I was the bigger boy of the two of us, but then Roy fell on me and pinioned my arms to the grass with his knees. "How dare you go in our house when we aren't home," he said, and I said, "I'm sorry," and felt it coming. Roy acted like he was going to hit me, but his fist never came, only the hurt.

SHE LIKED MY CAR

SHE LIKED MY CAR, nothing fancy, a Corolla by Toyota that was clean, dependable, and the light blue paint pleased her eye. I drove her to the coast in it. Along the way we stopped in a rinky-dink town where she bought an old dress from a country lady glued to a stool. The dress was all greens, flowers on it, and back in the Corolla she stripped off her jeans and shirt. It was the first time I saw her naked. The wind blew in through the windows. The shadows from the pines made her skin flicker. I loved her ears. She climbed into the dress.

That was in March while she visited home during her break from Vassar, and she really liked my car. It wasn't a car I would have chosen for myself, but my grandfather died. My mother got my grandfather's car, and me, I got my mother's Corolla. I drove her to the airport in it. She asked me to give her hickeys, lots of hickeys to take back to college with her, so I did that, sucking her neck right there in the airport, and we both were happy.

A month later I'm taking a shower when this massive crash-bang shakes the house. I run dripping into the kitchen to see blue sky shining through a hole in the roof. Then I look through the window at my Corolla. It is totaled in the yard, squashed, crushed, completely destroyed. The pecan tree from the neighbor's yard gave up the ghost.

So Shane sold me his ancient Econoline van with bad brakes. It was dirty inside and veered all over the road, sometimes starting by itself in the yard or while sitting in a parking lot. When my girl graduated from school, I picked her up at the airport in it. She didn't like the Econoline as much as she had the Corolla. It was early June, very hot. We ate apples as I drove us to the shotgun shack that I rented. I pulled us into the yard. I killed the engine. We started kissing. She was wearing the green dress with the flowers all over it. I unzipped it in the back. I peeled it off her in the hot cab and we made love with her bent over the corrugated engine cover, also called a doghouse.

She moved in, but I'm a junky kind of guy and she is quite the classy woman. She missed my Toyota, and in the years that followed she climbed her own ladder of cars, trying to reach that flowery height of Toyota Corolla bliss. She bought a cheap green Honda that smoked. Then she bought an awful gray Honda lemon. After that she moved up to a Toyota Tercel, which wasn't nearly as good as the Corolla, but closer. Now she drives a silver Saturn, which is closer still. It's dependable and clean, but it's not the same. That Toyota Corolla was a really good car.

INTENSIVE

DUNNY WALLENSACK plays hacky sack under the mango tree, the girls his charge, the girls colorful in shorts and skirts, in sandals, a dewy brood from the middle class, what Dunny will chaperone through the great Mayan ruins. Oh, they will eat tortillas and climb a pyramid built around a pyramid and throw coins into the sacred hole of the water god. They will spin. They will run. They will drink cold Coke in the sunshine, and so Dunny laughs. He ankles the sack while upstairs at the Iguana Verde. Jeannette says to Cowboy, the only boy on the intensive, "Comb my hair." In her palm is a green comb.

Cowboy sets his mango seed on the blanket. He wipes his fingers on his jeans. He takes her comb. Jeannette plunks down beside him. The ledge of the bed sinks. Cowboy runs the comb through her hair that is long and brown save the last three inches where Jeanette dunked her ends into a cup of Clorox bleach. Her bright ends give her a punky look.

"You want to get high?" Jeanette says

"Wait, what?"

"You know me."

"You mean?"

"Yeahp."

"What would you have done, though, like if they searched your bags?"

"They can search my bags."

"You mean?"

"Yeahp."

"I bet it's uncomfortable."

"Not so bad."

"My God, you could have been in prison for five years!"

Cowboy works her snags. The comb starts running free.

"Let's roll one up," Jeannette says.

"What about papers?"

"I've got tampons."

Jeannette gets up, goes and locks the door. She grabs her clutch off her suitcase, pulls out a tampon and gives it to Cowboy. She quickly gets out of her jeans and sits on the bed and brings a leg up. "See." She pulls out the sandwich sack. It is thick inside with green buds her father grew.

"Wow."

"You wanna eat it?"

Cowboy picks up the wet mango seed and rubs it between her legs.

"Oh shit!" Jeannette throws her head back.

"What?"

"You know what you're gonna have to do now, don't you, Cowboy?"

"Wait." Cowboy turns the seed the other way and slips

it in. Jeannette pushes it back out into his hand. He squeezes it in again. In and out the orange seed slides.

"Goddamn it, Cowboy!"

"Free baby! Free baby!" Cowboy says, laughing.

Jeannette is laughing.

The door knocks.

Jeanette stands. The seed slides slimily down her thigh and plops to the floor. "Hide the weed," Jeanette says, and steps into her jeans. She opens the door. The girls come in and look Jeannette over. They look at Cowboy.

"Howdy." Cowboy raises his wet hand as though being sworn in to a court proceeding.

Jeannette grabs the tampon off the bed.

"We're going for a walk through Merida," one of the girls says. "You coming?"

"Soon's I put my tampon in."

Cowboy walks out onto the balcony, the sack of weed in his pocket. He steps over to the next room where his biology teacher, Dunny Wallensack, drinks from a bottle of tequila while dancing on the rug and singing, "La cucaracha! La cucaracha!"

"Howdy," Cowboy says.

"Swig?"

"Sure."

"Don't tell."

Cowboy turns the bottle up, swallows three good ones. He sets the bottle on the dresser, wanting to gag, but smells his fingers.

Dunny Wallensack laughs.

"What?"

Cowboy's teacher pats him on the back. "Cowboy," he says, "there's no reason you can't fuck them all. I'd do it myself, especially Dina, but can you imagine if I was to fuck Dina? I'd feel like I was having incest, and not only that, I'd probably split her in half."

Cowboy leaves his teacher's room and stands on the balcony, looking down upon the mango tree whose boughs sag with fruit. It is late afternoon, the light orange and yellow. From the street singing floats over the courtyard wall, propelled through the air by strumming guitars, a violin. It is Cowboy's last year of high school, the end of it, and the burn of the tequila mixes nicely with mango taste and the smell of Jeannette's cooter. Cowboy just stands there, looking at it all while beyond the wall a legless man pushes through the street on a skateboard. The man wears a shirt that says, in English: I CAN DO ANYTHING.

BUMPY

FIVE DUDES IN A VAN pick me up off the side of the highway. They are nice enough dudes, on their way to a Grateful Dead show, but one speaks of the great sensations eating a banana will give you. Would I like to eat one? I think they've drugged my drink. Can't say I like the setup, so when we stop for a piss break I run my life off into the woods. I spend the night slogging through moonlight tripping. Come dawn I'm curled up on the edge of a field. A tractor wakes me. This farmer dude hops off the tractor, says he is Thomas, will I work for him? I'm like okay and Thomas tractor-rides me to the farmhouse where I meet Sharon.

Talking to Sharon, Sharon pulls a pack of Oscar Meyer Wieners from the fridge. Her fingers look nice pulling a dog out, nails white and varnished. She bites it but a bang comes from above, sounds like an animal. There's this growl and a pounding and yowl, so Sharon sidles to the foot of the stairs. She pauses to eye me over her shoulder. "Come on and meet my baby."

I follow Sharon up the stairs, watching her ankles. They're nice, but Sharon stops at a padlocked room in the hall, leans over, uses the key on her string-necklace. When the lock snaps free the growling stops. "Bumpy know we here," she says, and we go in.

Wearing nothing on the bed is this black alien with a conehead. His eyes bulge out inches from his face, and he is weighty, I mean with breasts, and there are pink peeled-away places on his face. He doesn't have much of a nose, and his hands and feet got no fingers on them—they are paddles, poor thing. And the dick—I guess it's a dick—sticks out from a hole between his legs, and he doesn't have any teeth to speak of. His mouth is wide open. That's how I know. About the teeth. He looks at me dreamy-eyed, a string of drool seeping from the cleft in his huge fat bottom lip, a lip that, I notice, is pinker where it rolls down into the spit trough.

Sharon throws a hotdog on the bed and the thing grabs it up with a paddle and swallows it, all of it, all at once, the whole thing gone in a flash.

"Well," I say.

"He got some problems."

Sharon throws Bumpy another dog, though this time she throws it into the corner of the room. Bumpy jumps off the bed, grabs it, it's gone. Bumpy jumps back on the bed and jumps up and down on his paddles and knees. "You want another hotdog, Bumpy?"

Bumpy looks up at the ceiling and howls. Sharon holds out the dog. Bumpy sucks it up like a string of spaghetti. Sharon reaches out, scratches Bumpy's head. I say, "How old is Bumpy?"

"He five," Sharon says, and as she scratches Bumpy, the noises Bumpy makes are like pigeons, how pigeons coo, only louder. Bumpy's paddles start grabbing at Sharon's dress, pulling at it, his eyes bulging out wet-like and pathetic as anything. I see there is a real person inside there.

Bumpy keeps paddling at the straps of Sharon's dress, and Sharon keeps pulling her straps back up, slapping Bumpy's paddles, trying to get Bumpy to stop paddling her. No matter. Bumpy's paddles paddle right straight back and grab, and Sharon scratches Bumpy's head more, or cone, I should say. Bumpy likes that. Bumpy nudges the tip of his cone against Sharon's breastbone, jabbing her and pulling away so that she can get better leverage, more scratching in, and when Sharon scratches, sometimes Bumpy's eyes roll back into his head so all you see are the whites. I feel best when Bumpy does that because then he can't see me. But I'm jealous. My mother weaned me at four months. I guess I kind of hate her.

It occurs to me that I might should get back on the highway, "just keep truckin' on," as the Dead sing, but my heart is with Bumpy's mother. Bumpy's mother pats the bed for me to come sit.

Bumpy's mother looks like a thing I could eat.

I sit beside her.

Bumpy grabs at me with his paddles, the pigeon sounds in his throat increasing, growing louder, more excited. I don't think he is five. I think Sharon lied about that five business. Bumpy is more like some severely retarded thirty-year-old—he is heavier than me—and the sounds in his throat, that weird cooing, get louder as Bumpy grabs my shirt, twisting it in his paddle as though getting me ready to pummel. I don't fight it. I just let go. And Bumpy does the same to his mother, twisting her strap with his paddle and breaking it. Sharon's breast plops out and she laughs, looking at me. Bumpy goes for the other strap. He yanks it and now both of her titties are exposed. He rolls his eyes up at the ceiling. He jumps down off the bed and coos quietly in his corner as I make out with Sharon.

That night at the dinner table Sharon and I shovel salted kidney beans into our mouths, but the upstairs growling and banging commences, this time twice as loud as before. Sharon's father, good Thomas who has spent his day harvesting tomatoes, pauses with his trusted fork midair. He cocks his head to get a better hear, then chuckles. He raises a brow while Sharon eyes me lovingly. I'm thinking golly, my God, is this possible? My mother said only a crazy woman could love me, but I can still feel Sharon's sweeping brown boob with its long-ass purple-hued nipple in my mouth. If Sharon is crazy, I don't care. I sucked the whole boob through my lips where it expanded inside me like a helium balloon. For a minute I thought it could wiggle down my throat and cause me to suffocate. I've never farmed before, only Bumpy, I think, is a pretty cool cat. With beans in my mouth, I picture myself walking Bumpy through the tomato fields. I see Bumpy hooked up onto the end of a chain. Bumpy is a big dude, as I say, a baby gone big, if you will. I see Bumpy tugging me across the field between rows of tomato plants, and I'm just running behind Bumpy, trying to keep up, you know, with Bumpy, and we're both laughing and having so much great fun. It's a life I could learn to love.

POLLEN

THE OWL WHOS and Lee's body opens. We name him
Elihu after her dad. A month later we're on the porch
under the dogwood drinking champagne in the spring
afternoon, the yard a-splash with watery greens from the
rain. Azaleas skirt the fence. They color the air bright
pink, white and yellow. "I told you I had some Cherokee,"
I say.

Lee downs her champ.

"He looks good," I say.

We eye him, there he is, snug in the baby swing,
squashy, ruddy, his hair a little burry. As far as I know,
the Cherokee people always had long flowing beautiful
hair. The hair of babies, I've been told, can be weird. "It'll
straighten out, it'll be like yours," I say.

"I'm not complaining."

"Why would you though? There's no reason to."

"I just said I'm not complaining."

"He's beautiful," I say.

"I know he is. Just look at him."

We are looking at him.

"I wish he didn't sleep so much though," Lee says.

"It's only been a month, come on."

"Don't babies cry? Why doesn't he cry?"

"He's well behaved," I say, and say, "Let me get a picture of you two."

Lee says blueberry skins might be stuck between her teeth from the pancakes I made earlier. "I think you're good," I say, and remember how much I love blueberries. Blueberries are such a great thing. I refill our flutes and say, "Here's to our little fuzz buster."

Lee sips, but her head, as it has done ever since we came out here to celebrate, swivels Elihu's way. We are both looking at Elihu. Lee's shoulders start jerking.

"What is it, Lee?"

"Nothing." She wipes her eyes with her palms.

"Don't say nothing," I say,

"Sometimes I think you are intentionally cruel."

"Lee."

"Thanks for ruining my birthday. Is that what you're trying to do?"

"Lee." I put my hand on her hand. "Look at the beauty out here," I say, and with my arm present our glowing backyard bristling with life and color and promise. "Doesn't the sight of it make you happy? Think how lucky we are to have all this."

Lee looks it over, but then looks back at Elihu. "I don't know," she says.

"If you don't know you don't know."

"You brought us there. You were there too. If it wasn't for you we wouldn't have been there."

"Our grand adventure."

"I regret it," Lee says.

"I know you do."

"And you don't, but shouldn't you?"

"When I look at Elihu, all I see is a beautiful child."

"No!" Lee says. Her eyes spill over.

"It's the pollen," I say. "When it's everywhere like this it clogs the air, you can see it clogging the air. It clogs our emotions too."

"Just shut up," Lee says.

I do that.

But then:

"He's a fine boy," I say.

"I didn't say he wasn't, goddamnit."

"Look how cute he is. He looks like your dad."

Lee starts up sobbing, not caring, it is what it is, but I see how her nipples have begun to seep, as if responding to her eyes, all of her a sad chorus of weep. Her tank-top soaks through with milk and just now don't you know Elihu bawls. Lee reaches for him. Her hands wrap around his body, and my heart lurches forth as if to stop her.

A GUY NAMED ALBERT

I DUCKED THROUGH the doorway into the fort where a framed Victorian hung on the sticks. In the picture grazed sheep and a barefoot shepherdess in rags held a staff. She looked peaceful staring over the fields, healthy and like she could never grow old. I wanted to be like her so took off my shoes. I peeled off my socks. I slipped off my jacket, wadded it into a pillow and got comfy with it on the bench.

Then she called for me. She was crunching through the leaves, coming my way in her puffy goose down overcoat, she with her bear, good ole Buzz.

I closed my eyes and began to snore.

They entered the fort. "I called your name," she said. "Why were you ignoring me?"

One wall of the fort held in it an upright tractor tire somebody rolled down the slope. Such are things. You walk through a wood you find rusted Model T Fords. Barrels and buses. Big rubber tires. "I'm talking to you."

I fell off the bench, smacking my lips and grumbling as though rudely awakened. "My gosh, I'm sorry, did you say something?"

"Never mind," she said in her bored voice; then: "How is this possible?"

On my side, still in the cold dirt, looking up at her, I said, "How is what possible, dear?"

"Don't act like it's nothing." She was getting testy, but she sat down on the log at the entrance.

I explained things, saying the builders explored the forest floor. They gathered up hundreds of sticks in their arms. They leaned their sticks against the fallen tree—its raised trunk was the fort's spine. I showed her how they stuffed the cracks between the sticks with leaves for insulation. The fact that I could explain it was sapping the locale of mystery, irritating her, so I cribbed my tongue. That's when she said, "What's Alzheimer's?"

I thought about this. My answer: "Long ago, many years before you were born, a guy named Albert was walking through the woods, turning his head back and forth like Buzz wiggles his butt back and forth." I waited for her to laugh. She laughed. I continued: "Everybody wondered what was wrong with Al, which is short for Albert, in case you didn't know. Finally somebody said, 'Hey Al, what is your problem?' Al said, 'Don't mind me, I'm just looking for my heimer. Have you seen my heimer? I really need to go to the bathroom but I need to find my heimer first.'"

"Heimer? What's a heimer?"

"Oh, you don't know what a heimer is? Sorry, I didn't realize. A heimer is another word for butt."

She laughed and made Buzz wiggle his heimer.

"When people get older," I said, "they sometimes forget things. People forget where their heimers are. This guy Albert became so famous for not knowing where his heimer was that they named the forgetting things disease after him. If you ever see a man walking through the woods in a hurry, turning his head this way and that way, good chance the fellow has Al's Heimer's disease."

She wiggled Buzz's butt this way and that way, back and forth.

"Why do you ask?" I asked.

"Mommy says she's afraid she's getting Alzheimer's."

"Ahh, I see."

"Do you think Mommy will forget where her heimer is?"

"No, but the thing is, when you get Alzheimer's, sometimes you forget who you know. Imagine looking at somebody you've known for years and not recognizing them or knowing their name, but they are talking to you like they know you."

"Oh my God, that would be terrible!"

"Sure would be."

"Let's go, can we go home now? I want to go home," she said. There was urgency in her voice.

"Sure, let's go."

We moved north along the forest floor, looking for a place to cross the creek. Instead we found a dead animal. Holding hands, she and Buzz and I stepped up to it. We saw the gouge in her side and the bone and frozen blood. A car might have hit her and she ran down here. More likely a coyote sunk his teeth in and ripped her open. Other than her wound, our fox looked normal. Her shades of orange and copper held strong, and her tail was bushy, her feet very black. On her face was a grimace, a snarly expression showing fear and flight, her lips curled in to reveal the teeth meant to scare off her attacker.

"I want to go home," she whined, and grabbed my arm with both hands.

It was getting dark, but we only stood there, staring at the fox.

COZY

THEY SLEPT in the golden straw, he in blue jeans and a pea jacket, she in a print dress of pink violets on green. In the morning he pulled the dress up to her throat and made love to her, only there were snickers. Looking over, they saw eyes floating in a crack between the boards. "Father!" cried the eyes, but it was too late. He shot off. They righted themselves. They strapped their packs to their backs then left the barn. On the hill stood a stone house from which an old man with a cane hobbled their way. They saw sheep they had not known were there the night before when they entered the barn. In front of them stood two little boys.

"We saw you!" one boy cried.

"Great, good for you," he said, and they hurried down the hill. Upon reaching the fence a rock hit her head and cut it open. They scrambled over the fence and ran. There was blood, but the cut wasn't so deep. There was a lot of blood. It inched down her face and dripped off her chin.

The cold was the problem. It was so cold and his ears hurt and they needed hats and she needed a Band-Aid.

They had wanted to visit the castle, but the castle no longer called out to them. The castle no longer interested them, for some reason, so they just said screw the castle.

Leaving Harlech, a shop popped up where doodads were sold, gimcrackery and snacks. The man inside the shop could not be called happy. The man inside the shop was downright cantankerous even. People are that way sometimes. Best thing is to let them be that way if they need to be that way.

"My girlfriend cut her head. You got a Band-Aid?"

"No," came the answer.

"Any first aid kits for sale?"

"No."

"How about hats? You got any hats?"

"As you can see," the man said, "I do not sell hats."

It was true. The man sold no hats. But a little quilted thing was draped over a toaster. He lifted it up and pulled it down snug over his ears. It was nice and warm. It made a good hat. He thought he'd go ahead and buy it but the man yanked it off his head and said, "That's a toaster cozy, not for heads."

She found it funny. It cheered her. "Not for heads!" she kept shouting, imitating the Welsh accent as they walked the cold road. "That's a toaster cozy, not for heads!"

But he could've used that toaster cozy. His ears were sensitive. He clamped his head between his hands. "Not for heads," he said, and her laughter soared, reaching him as though from far away, through flesh and muscle and bone. When he pulled his palms away from his ears, her voice rushed back in, louder than before, and he knew.

FAULKNER AT 110

FOR HIS BIRTHDAY the townsfolk read *Go Down, Moses* on the side porch of Rowan Oak where the man lived, where he smoked his pipe and wrote the books. Each reader reads for ten minutes, after which a bell is rung, and the next reader picks up where the last left off. I myself start reading at 9:40 in the morning, and it is quite the delightful experience. Finishing off "Was," and reading through the beginning pages of "The Fire and the Hearth," I am required to say stuff like, "I'll take that n****r," and "I'll bet you them two n****rs." When the bell rings I stop mid-sentence, take a seat in one of the ninety foldout chairs, and enjoy the view of the house while the reading continues.

It's a beautiful white box of a house, its eastern face a heaven-bound stepladder of painted planks, weather-warped boards and coated splinters. The six large mullioned windows of the upper floor catch lilac flashes and glimmer silver from the new morning, all this fresh

September air. The lace curtains of the two windows above the porch rustle now and then, and I keep looking for the hand of some gimp or child. The window is fogged, as if a ghost just exhaled against it. The shutters droop downward, and the gutters! Oh, the gutters! Rain gutters surround the overhang of the porch and run tubular to the ground; but the rain gutter most engaging is the one at the far right. It's close enough to the window to where a girl named Caddy might reach out from the sill, catch it and let herself down to the ground.

The reader up now is an old lady a bit squat with a snowy bell-shaped hairdo, aquamarine-framed glasses, the lenses large circles. She wears gold earrings and red lipstick and, "Lucas was just another n****r," she says, doing a fine job at it. When the bell rings I give her the thumbs up. She comes over to me, puts her hand on my shoulder and leans over, says, "I didn't have your good Southern accent," but you know, my accent is put on, hers is the real. Her perfume is nice, and the large padded breasts behind the black blouse press my neck. The reader up there now is a tall thin man, spectacles balanced on the tip of his nose. He says, "'I'm a n****r,' Lucas said, 'but I'm a man, too.'" And the curtains rustle.

Now it's a woman's turn to read—that's how it's going: woman, man, woman, man—and this one too is bespectacled with a shirt of red. "Fix him with sugar tit," says she, and I look at the freckled knee poking through the ripped jeans of the pastoral maiden sitting in front of me. She has a lovely neck, pearls in her lobes, and eats pastries from a white bag, licking her fingers. "His wife had removed only her shoes," reads the reader, and the girl wears pink flip-flops. Her toenails are painted pink to match the pink shirt she wears, her pink watchband, and the pink handbag on the blue foldout seat beside her. I lean forward to smell her, and the cedars move risibly in the breeze.

DUDE

DOF FEET thrilled him.

And vanity he hated, his mom's. He hated seeing sandals on men's feet—was not "mandals" the uncoolest word ever devised?—and conformity, poison ivy, roaches and lonely. Unfair cops he hated, and that people ate so much meat. Pierced noses and nose rings grossed him out, as did toe rings, yuck, soft sounds, the destruction of old neighborhoods, spoiled brats, underarm deodorant, or when his girl got sick. When his girl got sick he'd ask how sick she was, like did she need him to drive her to the hospital? She could never say. She seemed not even to know how sick she was. Finally she would get better, but he hated that. He hated how whenever anybody showed him attention she started coughing.

Some things about her, he admitted, he hated. Like her name, which was Lude—it sounded too much like dude, and dude was a word that reminded him of a whole slew of things he hated: jocks, football, Izod shirts, jeeps, creeps, bullies. His girl was nothing like any of that stuff, but still, when he called her by name, there was the association. Plus, Lude rhymed with rude, which Lude a little bit here and there was, and he didn't like being reminded of the fact each time he said her name. It made things difficult, so he started calling her Ludrilla, which didn't sound anything like rude or dude. Thing is, Lude hated being called Ludrilla, which in fact was the name given to her by her parents. Lude hated being called Ludrilla so much that she left him.

He lost his mind. He hated himself a whole lot after Lude left. He did not think he could live without Lude being near and dear, without having Lude around to talk to, or having Lude around to protect from the big bad crazy world out there, the scammers and poison snakes and scary people. It left him feeling empty, so suddenly he no longer hated Lude's name, but loved Lude's name— *Lude, Lude, oh Lude!*—and hated himself for ever having hated Lude's name, and for the stupid reason that her name rhymed with dude. He hated himself over all the bad ways he'd treated Lude, spanking her bare bottom in the bedroom, which he did sometimes, and for calling her "good girl," which was, Lude said, what you say to a dog after the dog takes a shit. He hated himself for winking at Lude—she hated that—and for having hated her lies when a woman should be able to tell every lie to her heart's content. He hated that Lude was gone, but Lude being gone was not the end of the world. Other things in the world gave him pleasure too, things that made up for the love and protection he wanted and needed now to give Lude. Things like playing guitar.

He loved playing guitar.

And loved making zines.

Hated Pearl Jam and Bruce Springsteen.

Loved crunching on salty greasy corn chips.

Hated how people spit on the sidewalks. That was just gross!

And he hated that feeling he sometimes had—it was worse than a death wish—that humanity was not what it was cracked up to be, that that "essential goodness" people spoke of was bogus, that when people said, "I love you," they never really meant it, and were mostly not nice.

Did he hate when people talked shit about Joyce Carol Oates?

Or Bret Easton Ellis?

That would be a big fat yes.

Even Larry Brown and Raymond Carver got dragged through the mud here and there.

As for King Sejong the Great, he loved the guy.

And hated lumbago.

Loved eating pussy.

Hated the world's history of cruelty and violence, or when people used the word "problematic" in any sentence.

It was so stupid.

He hated how people made him hate people, how people thought they looked cool while smoking cigarettes or walking around with coffee cups, tattoos on their arms. He hated how when people played music way too loud they either thought they were doing the world a favor or were pleased by the notion that their vulgarities would piss people off.

A lot of people, he had unfortunately noticed, hated silence. They came across a peaceful silence and they straightaway filled it with noisome garbage. He hated that, and hated them for doing that, for being obnoxious even though they couldn't help it—they were just that way.

He loved philosophy.

And Indian Pale Ale.

Hated when people said, "grown-ass man" or "grown-ass woman." How stupid was that? Some people, like his mother, even stooped so low as to use the word "ne'er-do-well" in reference to people she knew, like the sons of her friends. He hated the way envy could invade a person's face, and hated whenever a stereotype seemed made to fit. That was about as bad as it got. That really sucked. It really embarrassed him. He hated that. He hated mosquitoes. He hated knowing that mothers do not always love their children, or want them, even, to be happy as they get older.

Oh, but didn't he love riding his bike long distances through unfamiliar territory? He did! He loved homemade gravestones, goldenseal, sleeping outside under the stars, girl bass players, the smell of linseed oil, the smell of sewage coming up through the sidewalk vents when you visited New York City, walking through forests, bald women, reading biographies of interesting people and visiting the ruins of Southern slave plantations. He loved marching bands, even though they made him cry and cry, and Walmart culture most days of the week. Seeing women comb each other's hair was one of life's great delights. He loved the facial geography of "ugly" people, hot concrete under bare feet, and Asian women. Did anything under the sun beat Asian women? He loved hellfire preaching, watching YouTube videos, and Southern accents, fish sauce on Pad Thai, vinegar, Chelsea haircuts.

What he loved far outweighed what he hated.

Sometimes he described what he loved to people he knew. Their responses were like, "Dude, are you serious?" He would say, "I love smelling dog feet," and they would say "Dude!" He would say, "I love the smell of the waxy stuff that gathers behind my ear."

"Dude!"

Mostly he kept his likes to himself. He did not want people thinking he was weird. He knew he wasn't. He knew most people liked stuff he couldn't stand.

He hated their love of painted fingernails and fake fingernails and everything else that was fake: lip color, eyelashes, wigs, personalities.

He hated their hatred of rednecks and country people, and nor did he take to their habit of going around breathing loud all the time, grunting like hogs with snouts in the trough. Why did people do that? They grunted when they weren't moving hardly even. Though somewhat amusing, he hated when people cut their toenails in public, which they obviously loved doing. Or fingernails. He hated when people said bad things about broccoli and Brussels sprouts, stuff like, "the only Brussels sprout I ever liked was the one I didn't eat." He hated how his shyness often was taken for arrogance, his taste taken for snobbery.

He hated when people hated creativity, which seemed to be the natural course of things wherever creativity was concerned.

People who hated creativity made him feel awful, and Lude had sometimes seemed to hate creativity even though she liked being creative herself. When people were being creative around her, like playing saxophones or tap-dancing, Lude started coughing. Why did she always do that? What was so bad about other people getting attention? Did it make her think of the things she wished she had but didn't? He didn't know, but he could see the envy invading her face. This too embarrassed him. Instead of being pleased by the successes of others, Lude wanted those rewards for herself.

Lude, though, was gone. So why did his heart race whenever he thought of her? It was *the lies*, and fact that Lude used her name, the thing about how he'd called her Ludrilla, as an excuse to leave him when what she really was doing was leaving him for a richer dude, for Lude, during the years they were together, had come to love diamonds and Jack Daniel's and dinners at Brown Derby. The stuff gave Lude pleasure. It was OK to love that stuff—of course it was okay—just don't say "I love you" to anybody, please, unless you mean it.

Lude loved fashion magazines, fancy panties, beauty products from well-known companies. She loved screaming at him and pulling his hair and saying ugly things to him. It was OK, really, she could beat on him if she wanted, and bash him with a baseball bat, no problem. She could be hateful, it was OK. She hated his feet. They were too soft. And Lude hated his eyes whose lashes were too long. Lude hated, even, that he loved the smell of dog feet. Once, when they were out walking, he knelt down to smell some strange dog's foot. She said, "But what if there's shit on that foot?" and he said "Dude," like why must you worry about such things? Like his mother, Lude hated that he was not ashamed of the things he liked. Just how could anybody smell a dog's foot.

THE VIEWING

THE NAMES of the women make great reading—Kathy Cotton, Torsha Walton, Gesenia Mason—but what they write disconcerts you. All so many God Bless Americas, gag me with a spoon. Lexie Lasher has put down, "My heart cries," and Ursula Bliss, "God has 3000 new angels." A woman named Mary Xmas wrote this on the wall: "THERE ARE NO GODS, THERE ARE NO MESSIAHS, THINK INSTEAD OF GOING TO WAR." She's put A's for Anarchy in all of her O's. A little different, but still embarrassing.

I'm sad. The man in front of us has tiny American flags all over his necktie.

Then there's Yumi Card from Vermont who wrote: "WHEN YOU COME HERE, DON'T JUST STARE AND TAKE PICTURES."

It reminds me that I need to take a picture of the woman I met an hour ago while standing in line at the South Street Seaport to get my ticket. *She* is Nozomi. We walked over here together. I like her pointy face, how short she is. Her skin tone is the cheese. And I like the *all too human* breath that comes out of her, how it washes over me now and then like some warm breeze blowing across a field of tilled earth mixed with compost.

"Say, is it okay if I take your picture?" I say.

And she says, "Yes, yes, take it," so I take it, *cha-ching*, and the line frees up. Nozomi and I are admitted. We hit the deck and *hey hey*, there it is, the big to-do, a wide-open space, not so spectacular as one might think, a gash in the ground is all, a hole of wreckage crowned by buildings mutilated and scarred. Looking back and forth from the rubble to Nozomi's awesome face, I flash on a bomb going off, and see thousands of Japanese women—*no, tens of thousands*—getting wiped out by flames. A burning arm sweeps through the city, jealously gathering the good stuff up. Can you smell them burning? Their flesh is on fire. It happens. It *has* happened. A grand barbecue. Asian cuisine.

Like the hair commercial used to go: *Don't hate me because I'm beautiful!*

Or because I'm rich and powerful and large.

Cranes hoist slabs, trucks haul rubble.

Enjoy the evidence while you can.

They (us Americans) have been thinking of what to put here in its place. Nozomi says holograms are on the table, true-to-life holograms of the towers are a serious consideration, and she would know, having been on a committee in art humiliation, I mean, art administration, where the options were discussed. Nozomi has the loveliest nose. Each time I see it I get this impulse to either bite it right off her face or give it a nice little kiss.

On the rail somebody wrote: BIN LADEN CAN SUCK MY BIG FAT DICK.

It's weird is all, how we (us Americans) are more horrified by this than the Jorge Vidella stews and the sugar cubes of the Khmer Rouge. The Allende milkshakes of the world don't much interest us, nor the cherry-filled Tutsi Rolls or Croation croutons. We mourn only for our own, and only for those in our time. Yesterday is history. It feels wrong, so allow me to honor instead the million dead of the Viet Cong.

They are pulling bodies from the hole. Ten they will get out today, decomposing, bones showing through, rat-eaten.

It doesn't move me.

So I kick things up a notch, stick a towering Buddha in the hole, *hey hey*, a monster of living stone who smashes a golden gong with a liquorice stick of bent steel. As the gong reverberates, a hundred thousand naked Asian hotties fall bleeding from the sky, burning and flapping their legs as though they are wings. They are trying to save their lives by flying but all they can do is fall, fall, fall into the hole. Their screams and the expressions of agony on their faces and the splat sounds of them landing in the rubble pains me so bad. The emotional overload makes me grow backwards until I am a child again who knows nothing of the whys and wherefores of the world. In a Rubber Ducky voice, very loudly and retardedly for everybody around us to hear, I shout: "Mommy, is that the place where you were talking about, where somebody died?"

Faces pivot our way, and my great new friend, Nozomi, puts her best foot forward. "This is the place,

Baby," she says, and it could be my mother talking to me, my pointy-faced mom here with a sizzling bod. Nozomi stands on her toes to pat my shoulder.

The faces, the people, they shift uncomfortably in confusion. But I'm only a retarded kid—they see this—a baby gone big—and so do not castigate me or my wonderful mommy. I am everybody's friend. I say, retardedly and loudly and tremulously and filled with fear to Nozomi, "Where's the dead body, Mommy?"

Nozomi says, out loud for everybody: "The Lord has him."

And I heave out a great sigh of relief.

The eyes watch us, and the people give Nozomi looks of approval, as if she is doing a great job mothering her challenged child, never mind that I am older than Nozomi and hope to get into her panties later. She's got my hand in hers, and tugs me along, away from the destruction, away from the people looking down after us, and then looking back down over the rail where the destruction is. In this gentle tugging, in this walking away that we are doing from the people on the viewing deck, we pass back by the names we saw such a short while ago—Gesenia Mason and good ole Torsha Walton. And there, again, is Kathy Cotton. I'm like, "Mommy, I want to write *my* name," and Nozomi reaches into her panties—I mean purse—and pulls out a sharpie. After writing my full name retardedly on the plywood wall, I write, beneath it: MY MOMMY IS THE BEST MOMMY IN THE WHOLE WIDE WORLD!

DANDRUFF

THE SUNNIEST DAYS you ever heard of were these, and hottest most humid—thank God Lois had a wall unit—where even the grass sweated, you could feel it on the bottoms of your feet. Like the day Lois on her day off of secretarying got a call from Fireball Roberts' Elementary to come get her daughter away from the other children.

We drove out there. Inside of the school we were told by the lady in the office that Missy was on the playground, so we went there. Missy was the only one there. When she saw us she ran over to us but Lois put her hands up in a halting gesture. "Stop! Don't you bring it over here."

Missy followed us, at a distance, to the car where Lois made her step into a Hefty Cinch Sack. My job was to close the top with one of those little twister things and use my finger to poke some holes out for Missy to breathe through. Once that was done, Lois said for me to put the bag in the trunk. I refused. I talked Lois out of it. It wasn't easy. It was like trying to move a paperclip across a table with my mind. It took all my energy. We argued in the parking lot for about ten minutes. Finally the bag shouted, "Hurry up!" All these children were looking out at us from the windows of the school. I went ahead and put the bagful of girl in the back seat of Lois's nice automatic Honda.

We stopped at Pic 'N Save on the way home for the medicinal formula. Then at the house all I wanted was to puff on a joint while sitting beside the air conditioner, but I had a job to do. I carried the bag out from the car, set it square in the middle of the yard and undid the twister thing. Missy's head popped right out. I told her stay, don't move, not a inch in case lice were falling off her and spreading into the yard. It was a stupid idea, nothing that would ever happen, only Lois had been freaking out all over on the ride home. Lois said lice stick around for years if you're not careful. You gotta stamp them all out, Lois said. Lois said when she was little her dad dunked her in the diesel tank used for treating wood fence posts and that Missy, in this advanced day and age, was lucky to get off so easy.

Lois was very specific as to certain measures needing doing. I did not agree with any of it, but since it's her place, her everything, her never losing a chance at reminding me of what a freeloader I am, I figured I'd be her pet, do what she says. I went to the garage, took off my shoes and socks and got the dog shears hooked up to the extension cord that I dragged out into the yard with me. That's when I noticed the grass sweating. It was ridiculous. I thought, weather like this should be reserved for demons in Hell!

I shaved Missy's head. I told her she heard what her mother said. It was dumb. Missy didn't want to. I never would have had I been her, but she looked at the window and there was Lois looking like, *You'd better if you want to come back inside.* So she did it. I squirted a circle of blue medicine around her clothes that were in the grass now, including her shoes and socks and the clumps of long blond hair I had gathered up and put on top of it all. That was to, as Lois said, create a poison barrier so the lice could not escape. Each time I turned my head I saw Lois looking out at us from the living room window. She was in there safe and quarantined, enjoying the air conditioner and making sure everything was done right. She brought this glass of iced tea to her lips, took a sip and smiled.

I squirted blue medicine onto Missy's bristly bare head, scratching it around on there. She was crying. I felt shitty for doing this. On the bottle it said you didn't have to cut the hair off. I'd told Lois that, but Lois said no, uh-uh, directions never told a thing about the right way of doing a thing. "You have to use your brain," Lois said, and tapped her forehead.

So I was making Missy cry. I said, "It'll grow back," but Missy cried more. "Look," I said. "Don't cry. It makes me want to cry too."

"I don't care," Missy sobbed. "I hate you!"

"Look. Didn't I just say it will grow back? You have to be patient."

"I don't want to be patient," Missy said, stomping her foot. "I should run away."

A breeze blew, not a breeze like it is that a breeze makes you think about, all that cool refreshing air brushing against you, but a hot breeze where you feel the crazy heat in it sucking the blood out of you. Then there was a tapping on the window. I stopped scrubbing Missy's head, my hands resting in the blue lather on her scalp. I looked over to see Lois looking frantic. Her lips were moving, but all I heard was a muffled impatient sound mixing in with the straining dripping hum of the wall unit. That, and the little sobby noises Missy was making. I read Lois's lips though. They were going, "The bag! Get the bag!" I turned my eyes to where she was pointing and saw the bag Missy had been in parachuting down the street. I looked back at Lois. She was angry. "Get the bag!" she kept saying from behind the glass, her eyes growing bigger and bigger. I looked at the bag. It was way on down the street now, sailing along. I looked back at Lois. "You want me to get the bag?" I said silently, moving my lips only. "Yes!" she screamed. "The bag!"

So, I don't know, I felt weird leaving Missy in the yard—the blue lather was running down her back now— but also I wanted to get this over with. I took my hands off her head, shook off the foam and started after the bag. That's when I realized how hot the street was. Burning. It was burning my feet. My God. I started leaping to minimize the contact my feet were having with that road. It wasn't working so I ran along in the sweating grass of our neighbors. I was making progress, getting right up to the bag. I was about to snatch the bag, but the bag took off, upward to where there was no way I could get it.

The bag sailed high in the hot wind, ballooning over the houses and dropping out all those little lice and lice eggs, millions of them. The entire neighborhood is going to be infested, I thought. This is a serious situation! Call the National Guard! I watched the bag sail over a house with all these pink plastic flamingos stuck in the yard. Then it disappeared, falling down somewhere over there, but hell if I was going after it. I was tired. I was breathing. That's when I noticed a whole mess of bags looking like the bag I lost. The bags were filled with leaves and yard clippings and piled up in somebody's trash. Great! I went over and emptied one out. An old lady came running from the house. I ran. I didn't care. I had the bag.

First thing I did once back in the yard was wave the bag for Lois to know I had captured it. Her face took a sip of tea and she looked very pleased and proud of me. I went to the garage, got the can of gas we use for the mower, and went back into the front yard. I wadded up the bag and nudged it under the little pile of clothes. Missy was saying something, but I wasn't listening. I didn't care. I knew Lois was watching. I was going to do this the right way, use my brain, clear Lois's mind, erase it like a chalkboard with all kinds of crazy math problems on it.

Sweat was dripping off my forehead, flinging off my nose as I doused Missy's clothes and shoes and hair with gasoline. Soon this would be over. Soon the bald girl and I would be inside out of the sun, enjoying the cool air, me drinking a glass of apple juice and puffing a fat one, she whimpering over lost beauties. "Step back," I said, and dropped a match on it and it went up in flames, a big black ball of smoke rising up, up, up until it blended into the air. It might seem silly, but I squatted by the fire. I held out my hands, warming them on the flames. There's something about flames, they make you want to warm your hands on them.

Missy didn't like seeing me taking it easy. "It stings," she said, so okay, I picked up the box of Rid-A-Lice and a little green comb dropped out. Oh shit, was I supposed to use that? I started reading the directions. Oh shit, it said in capital letters: DO NOT LEAVE FORMULA ON FOR MORE THAN TEN MINUTES. I knew it had been more than ten, but I had to use the comb. I had to make sure. I grabbed it up and quickly ran it over Missy's head. Then I went and got the hose. I put my thumb over the end and sprayed Missy's head. She didn't like it one bit. I told Missy about the towel waiting for her in the garage and she ran off dripping like that girl in the picture where a bomb exploded. That's when I felt this terrible itching on my head. I started scratching. At that moment I caught a glimpse of Lois. Her round face hadn't moved from the window. She was looking at me suspiciously, like maybe she didn't want me to come into the house just yet. I almost felt like making a nasty face at her, because forget it. I was not going to shave my head over this. I don't care what her dad did to her, she can keep her dad, and all her memories of the shitty things he did. What business is it of mine? All I want is peace, a big fat joint now and then without Lois breathing down my neck. But no. Lois started shaking her head. "It's dandruff," I said, moving my lips only. I don't know why I would ever do that, move just my lips only, but I did. I said, "I don't have lice." And that's when I saw that old lady coming down the road as if she was going to tell on me about having stolen her bag.

BOULDERS

YOU'LL THINK you hear thunder, but the mountain is weeping—her boulders are tears; they tumble down her cheeks, rumble and flail and smash apart against granite, echoing through trees, over plume and across the valley. Of our land of rain, we say, "It rains," but sometimes our clouds dry up and we see stars, red crystals turning in the sky, a soundless menacing beauty. Nor are we fooled by the allure of glaciers; and check out those emerald humps beyond the canal over there; they wait for the butts of cartoon giants in ten-gallon hats—*saddle up boahs!* Raise your eyes. Do you see the eagle with a bagel in her beak scavenged from the Superbear dumpster? Ravens gurgle. Crows clutch berry clusters in scraggly trees by the post office; they look hanged by nooses. They bite, thrash, use their weight to break free. These crows land gracefully then peck at the ground, enjoying berries.

Last week a boy from Texas arrived by pleasure boat. His parents were treating him to a tour of the Inside Passage.

The boy saw killer whales, icebergs, colored fogs and snow. When he saw our mountains, he told his dad he would go find something strange and beautiful. He told his mom he would be back for supper. He made for the slopes. He climbed a good ways up, clinging to the mountain in the manner of a spider, but he slipped. He fell into the boulders far below. A team came out to clean up his brains.

He is not our first dead tourist. We have had copter incidents, people cutting legs on ice, avalanche victims. One lady fell down a mine shaft. The boy from the Lone Star State had just graduated high school. That's why he was here, to celebrate the possibilities of his future. We tell these people that if you see a bear walking along Gold Street, please, do not try to pet it, but they are hungry for stuff that is new. From the decks of the boats they see the colors. They see the tour busses and tramway and wood cutouts of salmon fishes and think they have arrived in paradise, where they cannot be harmed.

As with each noteworthy thing to happen in our town, we discussed the Texan's death at the Alaskan Hotel and Bar over pint glasses of Pale Ale, locally brewed. We felt for the parents. The boy had been on the football team. He was in the equestrian club, had graduated with honors, had even been prom king. All this was revealed in the paper.

What our town took from the boy's parents cannot be atoned for, ever, so we pitched in for a plaque with their son's name engraved on it. On the plaque we included a brief account of "David's" short adventure and, as the mountain wept, nailed it to a spruce tree in a spot boys of a similar mind might happen upon. We hope these boys pause here, and take a deep breath before continuing their quest for something strange and beautiful.

AJAX

AJAX SNORTED it first off then shot it, played guitar, discovered the sax, smoked Camels unfiltered and fucked the fiddler's daughter Cindy. The fiddler was asleep by the fire, drunk, when they did it in the house. It was their first time. Ajax left Cindy on the mattress, stepped outside and peed into the fiddler's beard. For that he got kicked out of the band and suffered weeks running—but the stuff's no good for you, Ajax decided, and smoked away and cried a lot. Ajax thought back on his first time. He'd been in the empty tub naked a full hour, jabbing, making a huge mess of his arm until he figured it out. For a beautiful thing to enter the heart, it must be aimed at the heart.

A plastic surgeon hired Ajax to mow his lawns, plant flowers, bushes. But Ajax had moles on his back. The surgeon cut one out. The mole was sent off, analyzed, and returned. "Now you know," the surgeon said.

Ajax ran into the fiddler in the coffee shop one day.

The fiddler thumbed his nose at Ajax. Ajax realized then how great the fiddler was. The fiddler had taught his daughter Cindy all his licks. Cindy played violin in a punk band now.

Ajax joined the Hare Krishna Brotherhood, became a vegetarian. The touchy-feelyness of the group reminded him of his mother who, while he was in high school, ordered a fuck swing that arrived in the mail. She attached it to the ceiling in the living room. She gadded about naked. Ajax still had a key to the house, but never visited. He was terrified of coming home to find his mother and Gary going at it in the swing.

Gary was all right. Gary sang dorky songs for children, that is what Gary did for a living, went school to school playing guitar and singing *Jimmy Crack Corn* and *Give A Dog A Bone*. Ajax's mother no longer played guitar. She gave it up the day Ajax broke it.

Ajax remained a vegetarian until he met Suni, a Muslim woman of extraordinary blackness who'd drunk maté in half a dozen South American countries. Ajax found her in a corner of Lafayette Park deep into a candlelit prayer session, her ass up high in the air.

Ajax married Suni, followed her to North Carolina, to Asheville where her father and Muslim hub was. Ajax ate burgers from McDonald's. Sometimes Suni slapped him hard across the face, but he deserved it. Saxophones were evil, the voice of death, she said. If only she could be still long enough to listen through a Johnny Hodges tune, front to end, Ajax thought, she would understand. Suni threw the library records into the trash. Ajax sold the sax.

When the 9-11 thing happened Ajax and Suni watched on TV the fiery explosions, those planes crashing into the buildings, those people perishing under the weight of a million tons of concrete and steel. They hugged on the couch, frightened, but Suni made a chicken curry that night, her best ever.

Now Ajax works in pest control, visits houses in rich neighborhoods, exterminates roaches. In the kitchen of a plastic surgeon, Ajax listens to the surgeon speak his mind: "What they ought to do with this Bin Laden character, when they catch him, is drop him out of a plane a mile above the earth. That way he'll have plenty of time to think about what he's done as he drops into hell." Ajax nods, and squirts juice into the corners of the man's kitchen.

PAM

WHAT FASCINATED ME about Pam, and what made me want to marry Pam, was Pam's passionate hatred for human beings. Pam hated all human beings, they were all the same, they ate meat, they took advantage of animals. Pam wanted a planet with no domesticated animals. In the past Pam had eaten meat, yes, but what could Pam do about it now? In retrospect, Pam's meat-eating was a terrible mistake. As for the caterpillars Pam periodically steps on, which fall in droves off the side of the house onto the concrete slab outside our front door, if she can't help it, she can't help it. How much better it would be were those caterpillars human beings!

It is just remarkable how Pam has matured. At one point Pam liked feminists, but now Pam hates feminists, thinks feminists are ridiculous. Feminists are touchy-feelies, university people, post-graduate proletarians, people she does not want to socialize with: ghouls, fairies. Worst of all, feminists are humans, and like all humans, are unclean, filthy. What had begun early as a suspicion has, with age, crystallized into a beautiful certitude.

Look, I've got Pam's travelogue from our first trip to Mexico, way back in 1982. I saved it because I thought I might be able to use it one day. Just listen to this. Pam titled it "A Chemist's Approach." Here goes: "Seeing human history in terms of primary elements in multitudinous combinations, transforming, mixing and rechanging again to form the entire panoply of social formation and cultures that have ever appeared on earth. The Primary elements may be the pairs of man, originally pure and unmixed at the beginning of historical time. This primordial purity ended with miscegenation which presumably has been and continues to be the source of man's troubles. The solution is to return to the original apartheid, the apothecary shop, to separate out the elements, to break down the mix-breed molecules into their component atoms and keep them apart from one another for good." How do you like that?

So Pam, she's been good for me, even if she does call me a Kantian from time to time. "Stulb, you live by rules," Pam always says. Pam has always called me "Stulb," has never called me by my Christian name. It's Stulb this, Stulb that, why? Because I always called her Harper when she was my student. Now I call Pam, and Pam calls me Stulb, as does Gretchen. I don't like it, but what can I do?

I'm stuck. "How many days have you worn that, Stulb?" Pam will ask me.

"Two days," I'll say.

"Well, you be sure to put that in the dirty clothes this evening," she says.

It took Pam two years to get her nursing degree. She got her master's in Political Science afterwards, and could have gone on to get a Ph.D., but she didn't want to. Pam's chosen profession is that of a nurse. Pam's favorite part of the job is carting the corpses to the morgue.

It's an awful job. Fat people, so many fat people, having to roll them on their sides, having to smell them, clean them, touch them. Angry people, drug addicts; what cesspools of rotten humanity hospitals are!

Pam prefers the company of horses. She spends most of her time in the barn reading. She's an intellectual who buys her books from Borders, a super-intellectual but, if I tell her so, if I even mention the word "intellectual," I'm in big trouble, all because of that comment I made twenty years ago: "You can't answer me, you're not an intellectual," I said. I regret it every day because Pam knows how to hold a grudge. If Pam sees me reading, out of the blue she'll say it: "I'm not intellectual. I'm nobody. I'm just your servant. I do all the dirty work and you sit there and enjoy yourself." To that I say nothing. Once, I said, "Well, I've paid for everything." Bad idea. I hear that every day too. "You pay for everything." I say nothing in reply. I know better. Pam hates comments. I can't say this is a delicious meal, or what a nice thing you've purchased.

I, now that I no longer teach, now that I no longer drive Gretchen to school to attend her classes, have nobody to talk to. Gretchen, having spent all of June in Prague attending a music symposium, has gone off to some dopey college in Augusta to learn her math. When Gretchen comes home on the weekends she doesn't talk to me anyway. She's up to her neck in schoolwork. She has earphones on all the time, even at the dinner table.

When she's not listening to music, she's practicing. When she's not listening to music or practicing, she's primping for two hours at a time before the fucking mirror. No, I have no relationship worth a damn with Gretchen anymore.

So, I hardly ever speak now. Conversation is dangerous. No comments, no retorts, no self-defense, no apologies, no bullshit. Pam tells me I'm a master of bullshit, which is true, but does that mean I should feel alienated from everything? I wish Pam would forgive me for my slips of tongue from the past, but that's not Pam. Pam remembers everything. Pam understands how horrible human beings are, and never lets me forget that I am human. These traits add up to Pam being the most trustworthy person I know. What a responsible, fantastic human being!

This is why I like talking to you, my favorite son, on these rare occasions when we manage to get together. I'd love to have you over anytime, but as you know, Pam will not allow it. You're not allowed to call me, either, but what can I do about that? If you'd like to get in touch, leave a message at the Philosophy Department, which I still visit occasionally to meet with my leftover dissertation students. This biography you're doing is all a secret. If Pam ever finds out about it, let me tell you, I will be a dead man.

FORTY

UP IN THE TREES lichens grow so I bared myself, why
not, and set my Sure Shot on timer, shot myself posing,
took the band from my hair, let my hair down (and let me
let you in on a little secret here: by typing I am trying to
irritate the guy who could have sat at any of the forty units
in the computer lab; he instead plopped down right
beside me so I pound the keys loud and fast and hard to
get the mother to move, get him to go!)—but OK, I was
taking pictures of me with nothing on. It was forty out,
lower maybe even but after climbing that high on the
mountain I felt warm. After taking this picture and that
picture my feet felt cold. The novelty of taking pictures of
me with nothing on was over, so I went and dressed and
smoked a cigarette. It was a nice time alone up there on
the side of Thunder Mountain. I got my shirt on then put
on shoes and started down, was on my way, headed for
the car, things moving along fine and dandy, but here
come to find out the trail runs into a Devil's Club patch,

smack into the patch and things didn't look hot, things didn't look cool, things looked thorny so I backtracked, found an orange ribbon thing wrapped around a sapling, what somebody tied there to guide you or warn you, I don't know, but this one seemed random. Back and forth in circles like this for an hour I went trying to see where I'd gone wrong, how I lost my way. That's nature. I panicked, the bowels got nervous on me. I said *calm down, bitch*, but had to go, what hell, so squatted and let it out and, get this, it's hard to believe but I actually, whilst shaplooting, unholstered my Sure Shot and reached around and snapped the stuff coming out, why not? Do you even know what your shplottle looks like oozing out of you? Didn't think so. But then again maybe you do. I don't know. But I started trying to get back on the trail. The trail though was no go, no luck, same thing, and then I felt all nervous again. I thought, *What if I die out here, have an accident and somebody finds me?* Think how embarrassing it will be when the person looks at the shots on my Canon. I took a moment to delete those pictures. The others looked good, I'm a good-looking guy, a better than average looking man. I would go so far as to call myself a downright exquisite creature, it's my proportions, I'm beautiful, delicate, aristocratic, I'm pretty, and the hair on my body, unlike the hair on most men's bodies, is not gross. I'm a thirty-nine-year-old lovepot is what, unendingly sexy, and lost, and stuck. While trying to get out of the woodsy tangle my hat kept getting snatched off by the trees. Seems I always get myself into tight squeezes, like here I am now hunkered down on hands and knees crawling through the lousiest terrain you can think up, not stickers and snakes this time, like what's usual for me when in Florida, but Devil's Club, Alaska stuff, the stuff gets stuck in you, small barbs that stay in for weeks, for months, and the sun was going down. I could not keep on this way forever so said fuck this shit and bushwhacked my way for the cars, the noise, the road, civilization, as they call it. It couldn't be all that far off, just who knew what kind of nasty trouble you might slip into along the way. I did it, though, all squishing and wiggling and stomping and stepping and crouching and crawling until what's this? A building, yeah, I was home free, all this garbage all over the place everywhere. People just love dumping garbage in the Alaskan wilderness. I kicked out to my car finally but I had lost my hair band. With my hair down I felt bummish, and wasn't I on my way to the computer lab at the university to get some stuff done? I was. I couldn't just waltz in, being a professor there and all, with my hair hanging down haywire, so I stopped at Fred Meyer, the big grocery store, and went in thinking I'd find a rubber band to use for my hair. In veggies there was the asparagus. Each cluster had nice thick purple bands wrapped around them. I didn't want any damned asparagus, so I slipped off the bottom band—there were two bands for each asparagus cluster, one on top, one on bottom—and when nobody was looking stuffed that bitch in my back pocket. Then I drove here to the computer lab. Everything was going along fine and dandy until, don't you know, *el doosho* here decided to sit down next to me. He wears a baseball cap, no less. I feel some animosity. I really should be more lenient when it comes to guys and their baseball caps. I guess I see myself as the center of the world, which I am, so can you blame me for having a great big log in my eye? I guess there are moments where I don't like people very much, especially if I am trying to get stuff done and some *el doosho person wearing a baseball cap* sits down beside me when there are like forty other units in the computer room!

WHAT HENRY NEEDS

ON THE PHONE Mom says they have piled up on my bed. She says they wait for me to return from school. She says, "Write him back, for crying out loud, tell him to stop," and says, "I've read about this, honey. They'll hide under your car while you're in the mall. When you come back to the car they will be under it, waiting for the right moment to reach out and cut your ankles."

"No, Mom! Just return them, okay? Throw them away, I don't even care!"

I see her. She goes to the box. It's filled with his letters all personal-looking and friendly, some with pictures or stickers on the envelopes. Mom takes his letters into the house, smells them, puts them on the kitchen table, telling herself she won't, no, she won't open them, they do not belong to her and, "Why didn't anybody write *me* letters like this when *I* was in college?"

I know Mom has opened them. She has opened them to see stupid shit like: *You are sitting lonesomely on a dry bank of a section of my brain staring solemnly at your feet that are in the river of liquid thought rushing by at a rapid pace headed downward to other parts of my body. It's a good place for you to be so long as your feet aren't removed from the water!*

Yes, that's verbatim!

And the cringe continues: *How sad I felt to read what you wrote—"I'm sorry I can't be what you want me to be." Don't be, you hear me? I'm proud of you as you are, my gosh, I practically broke down and died.*

And: *You said you loved me, remember? You said you wanted to be the best fuck I ever have.*

The crap don't stop!

You were!

Is he trying to lay a guilt trip on me? Does it sound like he cares? What he needs is a piece. Is it my fault he can't get laid? And true, I maybe might not should've said that thing I said, but what's there to do now? It was an in-the-moment thing. It wasn't the sort of thing I could have planned or thought out. I mean, since when are in-the-moment things forever?

What he needs is a blow-up doll.

Hey, if I send him one, will he forget me? I'll get a whole case of blow-up dolls, not just for Henry but for the men of my future. I'll get two, two cases of blow-up dolls so that I'll never run out. I'll drop a blow-up doll on the ground and kick it under my car whenever I go to the mall. This way I won't have to get down on my hands and knees like some dumb bitch looking under her car to see if some guy is there waiting to cut her ankles.

SCARECROW

SHE HATED his wink. She hated that damned wink. She'd be talking along and he would wink. And his shins were sharp enough to cut garlic with. He wanted to wrap that leg around her at night, but what woman would stand for that? He proved with a tape measure that she was five foot six instead of five foot seven. It gave him pleasure, didn't it? She hated his long eyelashes, his big lips made for kissing, these beautifully shaped little red pillows. There were so many things about him that she hated that she could talk on about it without repeating material. Whenever he tried talking about himself, her list of stuff shut him up. She was coming out of her shell. She enjoyed telling him what a selfish bedraggled scarecrow he was, how lost he was going to be without her. He blew it. He would not be able, ever, to look in the mirror because he would know he was just exactly what she said he was: a scarecrow.

NOODLES AND SOCKS

THE SOUP had two tiny dumplings in it, and approximately three thousand thick noodles. When an Asian tourist sat beside me and ordered it, I could've said what she'd get—*here, suck on this!*—but I wasn't feeling great. The Korean diners asked her, as they had me, where she was from. "Not China," she said. "I'm from Hong Kong." She pronounced her words slowly, her voice that of the boy Urkel, whom you might remember from that show called *Family Matters*.

"Ahhhhhhh," the Koreans said.

Urkel and I small-talked. She wanted to connect. As we both were alone, why not? I felt kinda sad when she screwed her camera into the end of a shiny steel pole, held it out in front of her and smiled, snapping off some selfies, chopsticks in hand over her steaming bowl of noodles.

I was full, even while chewing the damn things, and I said to myself, *Why are you doing this? Why are you eating these noodles?* I simply hated the idea of leaving food in the bowl for the *ajumma* to see, a real strong statement on what I thought of her cooking, eh? Finally I could take it no more, and maybe she'd recycle the unused portion. That was my thinking, so "I'm too full," I said in Korean—*nomu pebbuloyo*—and the *ajumma* did her magic trick, made my bowl disappear. I paid the 5,000 won. In my thank you I called her *agassi*, which means young girl. Her face darkened. She said, "Aigooooo," and told the other Koreans what I'd said. In Korean I said, "Look at me, I am a grandfather."

They looked me over, but no, I did not look like no grandpa to them. Though my hair was silver, my complexion was clean, shiny, a result of discovering sun block in my early thirties during the time I was married to a seventh generation Floridian who knew about such things. I was, in their eyes, *chal sengyossoyo*, or handsome.

After the noodles I walked around a ton of a bunch, the rain falling down out of the clouds making puddles on the ground that women in sandals stepped into while holding the hands of their daughters, who also wore sandals or colorful flipflops. The rain dripped from awnings, ran in the gutters. I stood upon an overpass watching its raised pattern dance in the Cheonggyecheon Stream that shot off into the distance where eventually it connected with the Han River before finding its way to the Yellow Sea.

I found my way to the subway. Rode the purple to the brown. Was carted to Itaewon where I'd lived for the last two months. I came here last summer too, don't ask why. My original reasons don't matter anymore. I just came. Last year I picked a few shells off the beach. All I took home with me were those shells and an empty carton of

Seoul Milk. It's the best milk. I love it. It's so creamy, so fortifying. Korean cows are fed different foods, or something, I don't know, but this time I bought some socks to take home. That's what I was doing at the Dongdaemun Market, searching for socks. After buying a ten-pack of socks scalloped nicely with ocher and navy-blue stripes, that's when I rewarded myself with the big bowl of "Dumpling Soup."

I got off the subway at Noksapyong Station. I walked up the hill to the room I'd been renting from a black guy from Ohio. Pardon me for mentioning it—that he's black—but blacks are not always treated so well here. He'd been having trouble finding fulltime work, so it pleased me to see him living the good life in his nice Itaewon apartment. He'd taught English in Korea for five years running, and wanted out now, only the prospects back home weren't so hot. This morning, while he was at work, his Korean girlfriend poked her head out of his bedroom while I was writing shirtless and sweating at the kitchen table. I hadn't known she was home. I made a small noise of surprise and she paused and I quickly slipped on my shirt and she stepped out and we talked a long time in the subdued light, she leaning against the sink in rumpled shorts and her face a little greasy from sleeping. She had lived in New York City for four years, she said, and wanted to go back so bad. Two days ago she came across a receipt stuffed in a book— it was for an expensive item she bought at the MOMA gift shop for a friend. She'd kept the receipt and the receipt made her nostalgic.

Her leg skin was peeling from a burn she got during a five-day vacation in the Philippines. She and her Ohio sweetiepie had stayed at the Shangri-La at three hundred dollars a night—that was for the cheapest room. I saw some of their photos on his Kakao Talk page. Under a picture of them drinking from the same coconut was the caption, "Say yes, please!" and I thought: in the Philippines he proposed. She told him she would consider it, but upon returning she found the receipt. The receipt had made the decision for her, and she was telling me now about the ex she left behind in New York. In the thing of it I told her of my ex who'd flown home to Korea from New York to be with her mother who was ill. Her mother died, and that was the end of us. Of course there's more to it than that, but . . . I did not say that my ex had lived in Woodside, the same neighborhood of Queens that she had lived in. Nor did I say that my ex pronounced the word "Woodside," as did she, without the W—*Ooodside*—which is to say *too cute for anything under the sun*. She wanted to exchange contact info. For some reason everybody wanted to connect today.

The Ohioan was home when I arrived, his door closed. I imagined him back there sulking, and was afraid for him. His beautiful, smart, Korean girlfriend with the good English speaking skills was everything to him. A deep well of sadness may have been waiting for him to fall down into and go splash in. I remembered how it was for me, my splash into the sadness. About my sadness my ex said what she said about all sadnesses of the world, that time solves everything. She was Catholic. We had talked of marriage. When her mother died, there was too much distance between us. Some stuff happened, and now she refuses to talk to me. The closest I could get to her was to visit her house, and take a few pictures of it.

By the door I took off my big-ass shoes then snuck into my room and pulled out my pack of new socks. The socks looked really good. I envisioned myself coming to love these socks in a very personal way. Perhaps one of my students would remark that I wore the same socks every day, and I would tell the story of how I bought them in South Korea during a pouring rain, then treated myself to a huge bowl of dumpling soup that was mostly just noodles. I was very excited to try these socks on, only as it turned out, they were too small.

HOW WE SOLVED THE PROBLEM

RACHEL GIVES UP RINGS and reading, gives up sucking my finger. I give up biting her toenails, not wearing underwear. No longer do I smell Rachel's short feet or lick her eyeteeth. Rachel stops mopping on her precious lotions, thank the Lord, her *Dermetics* and *Soothing Aloe Relief Moisturizer*. I put my camera down. Haven't snapped for a week. My hands feel off, ants all over my body.

Instead of eating up on peanut butter and Saltine sandwiches, instead of swimming, instead of making love through hot afternoons, we take these long-ass walks, like for miles. Today we cross the Halifax. We sit on a bench facing the Royal Steak House on Main Street, and watch folks walk through the glass doors for dinner. Everybody eating at the Royal is rich. Got ties on, suits, the women in fancy dresses and hats, the cars in the lot Buicks and Cadillacs. "I want steak," Rachel says. "You got enough? I want cow, real meat soaked in blood."

"Should I give up carrots?" I say.

"Slave," Rachel says. "The only way is to go all the way. Once we go all the way we can go back to before. You can take pictures again."

"All the way?" I say.

She didn't mean to say what she said, but she said what she said, is embarrassed by it.

I wonder what she misses more, my touch, or her bottle of *Jergens Soft Shimmer*.

"A riddle," I say. I say, "if you eat meat your pussy will taste like crap, but if you don't eat meat, I'll never drink your hot pink syrup again."

"Jesse, don't."

"But wait. You already are a carnivore. For a minute I forgot."

"Jesse," she says.

And I want to bite into her arm, taste her blood in the late afternoon sunshine. What she will feel won't touch what I felt. I don't touch her. I check my wallet. "All I got's enough for McDonald's," I say, and we head down the strip, cross A-1A, enter McDonald's. I order two Big Macs and a super-size of fries. It's gross, but it's gotta be done. We've decided. We take our tray to a table and, being Rachel's the meat eater, she goes first, denuding her burger with dainty fingers. Her mouth opens, even before she's brought the thing to it. Her lips pull back around her teeth. Before the stuff enters her mouth, I see the dangling thing guarding the entrance to her throat, a little bell ringing out the music of our lives.

PUSH ME DOWN THE LADDER

"You have the most beautiful face," he says.
"You look like you've been beaten," he says.
"Your breath," he says.
In his two rooms, a bathroom.
And kitchen.
In one of the two rooms they play Crazy Eights.
On the bed.
Burn candles, wax dripping down the walls.
And he whispers in her ear that a man comes along and cuts off her foot, boils her foot in a pot with organic carrots, and eats it.

"I'm wet," she says. "I keep getting wetter and wetter."

Close to her ear he whispers that he's going to photograph her with his Leica standing in the middle of a country road in Georgia, naked, with dead possums around her, and dead dogs maybe too, and dead cats, whatever they can gather from the sides of the byways.

The cards have spread across the bed.

"I'm going to put a frog in your mouth," he says.

Some cards are turned to the blanket. Others face the ceiling—some spades, clovers, hearts.

And they kiss.

But don't do anything more.

The next day he drives her to the forest, a wild lonely place with a sound of needles in the air.

He has a map to a hole in the ground, a secret hole that spews black water. A white fog is said to seep out of the hole and creep through the trees.

They come to an opening where a thousand flowers of every color grow, and pause before it, amazed, a large buck with antlers small on the other side the field.

Through the field they walk, careful not to hurt the flowers, and break into the forest where they see snakes, turtles, grasshoppers. Over logs they step, and through sticker bushes and high grass.

He'll never forget, he says, this moment, her cheeks bouncing and rosy in the light trickling down from the tops of the trees onto her face.

But the map.

Is confused.

They don't understand it.

Huts are in the trees, ladders going up to them.

So they climb one into a hut and examine the map, trying to figure out where they went wrong. She takes a few pictures of him with a disposable camera.

They are both sweaty because it's July and very hot.

And he says, "Tell me to push you down the ladder."

"No," she says. "I could die."

"Please. Say push me down the ladder," he begs, and smells her breath again, his nose going into her mouth, but she won't say it.

He grabs her, makes like he'll push her down the ladder anyway.

She struggles.

"No! Doesn't no mean anything to you?"

"Today is No Means Yes Day," he says.

"Are you trying to make me hate you?"

"Your boyfriend said things about you, you know?"

"He's not my boyfriend anymore."

"He said you like the tight fit."

"Huh?"

"That you stank up his bathroom from the onions. But *I* like *all* your smells."

"My God, I can't believe this is happening."

"Say push me down the ladder."

She won't, she refuses, and they never find the hole, nor do they see the white fog that might lead them there.

A sprinkle starts.

They make for the car through the sprinkle that turns to rain.

And thunder and lightning.

They run through the field of flowers, getting soaked and laughing and he drives her to his place.

Of the two rooms, the bathroom.

And kitchen where she peels her jeans off inside out and hangs them over the back of a chair to dry.

She gets onto the floor then, back to the fridge, rain tapping the roof, looking again beaten, overly elevated as a specimen of all that is great about humankind—impossibly there in the dim light. "Crazy," he says, and gets beside her. Cuddles on her and pulls at what's left of her clothes so she is naked, in a trance, the smell of rain and wet bark mixing with her sandalwood smell and smell of sweat and of hormones. How nice she's never shaved under her arms, ever, so he smells around more on her and licks. "Remember," he says, "that thing I was talking about?"

She doesn't speak, doesn't move.

"I have a cool surprise for you." He stands, opens the freezer door above her. He pulls out four garbage sacks, sets them frosty on the floor then reaches in the sacks and pulls what's in them out of them. On the floor now with her are two dead possums, a dead dog and five or six dead rats, a few with traps still holding them by the necks. "I've had an eye out for snakes," he says. "Been looking, but every snake I find is squished into nothing."

He screws his Leica into a tripod and sets it before her and takes pictures with a cable release. Directing her into a squat with her dead animals, he says, "Freeze," and she freezes. He tells her to look angry, to growl, and she does it, she says, because she believes in him. In this he has no choice but to lick her again. As he licks, she tugs his shirt, gets it off and he does the rest, is just fingering her now lightly, sucking on her neck, causing her to mumble stuff. He pulls back. "Huh?"

"Down the," she says.

He sort of pushes her over. Paralyzed into the dirty. Linoleum. Her feet go up amongst the furry creatures so he pushes her down the ladder. He's never pushed her down the ladder. It's the first time and, while pushing her down the ladder, she says, "Push me down the ladder," the animals around them frozen still, you can smell them, they are starting to unfreeze and smell awful but good too in a way. When they first met, she had said, "I don't eat murdered animals."

Smelling the smell more of them, she says, "Wait, stop," so he says, "Stop what?" and she says, "Stop pushing me down the ladder please." He says, "Really?" and she says, "No, no, push me down the ladder!" but he doesn't push her down the ladder because didn't she say stop? In their continued ladderlessness, she says, "Hey, stop not pushing me down the ladder!" so he pushes her down the ladder again. He pushes her down the ladder and pushes her down the ladder and then he pushes her down the ladder more, more down the ladder and pushes, pushing, pushing her down the ladder, the ladder, the ladder ladder ladder ladderyhxxv bybftdsaqk oppvbxd and pushing her down the and the and . . .

PILES

SHE LIKED PILES OF ROCKS and sawdust and silt. Whenever anyone asked about it, like why do you like piles so much, her response was, "I don't know, I just do," and she would laugh, thinking of her piles of shells, how her piles of dirt ranged from dark brown to gleaming white. Her only criterion for a pile to be a real true pile was that the pile, whatever kind of pile it was, was conical. She wasn't into sprawling piles or piles clawed into from opposing angles by backhoes. Overtly lumpy ant piles were not for her. The piles she liked, the ones she wanted to photograph, looked to have been poured onto the ground evenly from on high.

He admired her passion, her focus, her determination to assemble the greatest ever collection of piles. Because he also took pictures, it was the perfect friendship. They would park in the middle of some country bumpkin town then each go off on their own, he to photograph people he came across that he liked, and she, of course, to photograph piles. When they met back at the car at the

76

agreed upon time, they talked of their finds and it was always great fun to see each other's finds come to life after a bit of hard work in the darkroom. "Oh, that's that pile you were talking about," he would say, and she would laugh.

This was before the pains came, piling up on them, weighing them down.

He was eighteen, she nineteen. They both were in school. One day they crossed the Florida line into Georgia in her Datsun B210. Between towns she pulled over into the grassy shoulder and they stepped up into the pines. She peed in one spot while he peed in another. Then, still in the pines, they met back up and it was beautiful out everywhere around them. The smell of the pines was all so delightful that they took a moment to hug and to kiss a few nice long wet deep ones.

His hair was long, hers short. He went around barefoot a lot while she did Doc Martens. That's how they were while kissing in the scraggly woods alongside the highway. In the thing of it she got his jeans down and lowered him onto his knees, hiding him from the cars speeding by is all, only his face was in the needles. In this thing the tip of her tongue went where you wouldn't expect it to. His face was numb. She kept taking him to the edge, only to back off and cause him to whimper and push back wanting something deeper. In this way he bled into the world, becoming not himself, drooling into the needles where ants crawled, drooling as she tugged now, pressing in with her tongue while wrenching and twisting and yanking, working both hands. He came into the ants, their little shadows and the needles and was embarrassed.

Back on the road she again was filled with glee, brimming over with laughter, for with her, so many things had the potential of being funny. At the next town he went off his way, for the people, she off hers, for the piles. People and piles. Piles and people.

She had had a boyfriend once before, but she was his first girl. She was very likeable. She even had a gay friend about whom she told him the following story:

Her gay friend came home from the gay bar one night with a guy, but they both were too drunk to do anything other than sleep. When her friend woke up, he saw how the guy he'd come home with wasn't as good looking as he'd thought the night before. The guy had deep acne pits, "acne vulgaris," she called it. The guy started putting the moves on her gay friend and even though her gay friend wanted nothing to do with this guy now that he had seen him in the light of morning, they had sex, which of itself might not be worth mentioning, but here's the thing: while the guy with acne vulgaris slammed her gay friend from behind, her gay friend was watching an episode of *The Brady Bunch* on a small black and white TV. It was the one where Peter builds a volcano for school that's supposed to spew smoke and lava that runs down the sides of the volcano. Peter tries to activate his pile of dirt with a battery for his younger siblings but it doesn't work. When Peter comes back later with a bigger battery, Marsha is there with her friends from an elite club of girls called the Boosters. They have just accepted Marsha into their club. Peter plugs in the new battery and his volcano not only spews smoke, but dirty lava comes out of the volcano. The watery mud-colored lava splurts up into the air and soaks the girls in their short dresses, who are all mad at Marsha, but Marsha laughs and laughs.

Same as his girlfriend laughed and laughed.

The leader of the Boosters calls Peter a stupid kid, to which Marsha cries, "You wanna see something stupid, you should see your face!"

How could anybody not love Marsha Brady after that?

But he felt halted somehow, or weird whenever hearing her speak of her gay friend in such intimate detail. As their relationship progressed, and they started living together in the same apartment, she and her gay friend spent more time together. Her gay friend came to the apartment often, and it started to annoy him how they talked on and on while drinking plum wine and laughing. There was never an end in sight to the laughter so he would leave them and do other things. One evening after the gay friend left, she called him out on it from two rooms away. She said, "Why do you just disappear like that?"

The rooms of their apartment were connected by pointed archways instead of doors. He turned to her and said, "I'm not a fag hag like you."

At that she lifted off the floor on ropes—or so it seemed to him—and floated his way in a mad rush under the arches, her balled fist rising as she closed the distance. Full stop. She punched him in the face. They had just entered a deeper level in their relationship.

BILL'S BED

THAT IT WAS BILL'S made it more bad, the bed good for zilcho now. "Would you sleep in it?" he said, and I tired of his anger. What vexed me more still was Bill's ire with Zill whenever friends came over. "Your mom's a whore, you know that, don't you?" he would say, and then: "While I built this house to keep the rain out of your hair, your mom was off whoring in Disney Land."

The guys would look Zill over then at each other, their eyes saying, *It's a bit much,* and once, while we drank beer and smoked in the dirt, Bill even said to Martha, "Tell your daughter you're a whore." Martha said it. I'd never seen anybody look so humiliated. I felt bad for her, and Bill, for them all, even myself and those standing around who had to see it. Was it my business? No, but after Bill did his shotgun trick, blowing his heart out while sitting in the La-Z-Boy, I took up a room in the singlewide with its house-like attachment. As renter, I helped Martha with groceries and with Zill.

One day I came home early from hanging paper and Martha was in there in the master bedroom with Tyler, her cousin from the other side of the woods. The sound of them brought me comfort in the knowledge that Bill had been right. Bill had not been paranoid like people said. I started coming home early, same as Bill. I'd sneak into Zill's room while Zill was at school and press my ear to the wall. One day I heard Tyler say, "That's right, make it talk, make it sing like Elvis."

Another day I discovered a slit in Zill's moldy drywall. I stood on a chair and looked through it into the other room where Tyler had a flood light set up, and video camera mounted to a tripod. They were naked on Bill's bed, and Tyler said, "When I call you fat, act like you're offended. I want you to say How dare you call me fat? That's when I'll spit in your face and say Eat it, eat it, eat it like it's a plate of spaghetti and meatballs."

"Spaghetti and meatballs? I don't even like spaghetti and meatballs. Can't you make it something I at least like to eat? I mean, how about Boneless Chicken Piccata with Lemon and Parsley?"

"No, no, we can't have none of that."

"Why not?"

"Boneless? Really? In a movie like this, Martha? Are you kidding?"

"I don't want you spitting in my face neither, bitch."

"Goddamnit Martha."

Just then Zill came into the room and saw me standing on her chair, peeking through the wall at her mother. She said, "What're you doing, John?"

I put a finger at my mouth and went, "Shhhh," and got down off the chair and motioned for her to come outside with me right quick. Once we were a ways away from the trailer, I said, "Turns out your dad was right. I saw your mom on Bill's bed with her cousin in there."

Zill said, "I ain't never thought my father wasn't right. I sure miss him, but sometimes I don't miss him."

"Yeah, I miss him too, but you know what?"

"What?"

"There's no point in being woulda coulda shoulda about any of this. There's nothing we can do to bring Bill back. Just in case you're thinking you should hold this against your mother, I think it's best you forget about it and move on."

"You ain't gonna see me being no woulda coulda shoulda."

"Oh yeah? Why not?"

"Are you trying to take his place or something? Why are you even telling me all this stuff?"

"No, no, I'm not trying to be your dad. It doesn't seem like a very healthy environment for you to be living in is all. Your dad told me that Tyler was going to make a sex slave out of you once he and your mother killed him."

"He killed hisself."

"No, well, yes, but maybe, we don't know for sure, do we?"

"I'm the one who found him. Looked to me like he did it hisself."

"Yeah, but we don't know for sure, do we?"

"I don't need to know for sure. He's dead!"

"Okay," I said, holding up my hands, and we two went back into the trailer part of the house together. I poured some Cheerios and milk into a bowl for Zill while Bill's bed squeaked and bounced and banged against the floor in the other room. We heard slapping sounds and farting and slurping sounds and we heard Tyler call her fat. "I ain't fat you sonofabitch!" Martha said, and Zill laughed so that milk came out of her nose. A few minutes later, having heard us laughing in the kitchen, Martha came out from the bedroom fully dressed as though nothing peculiar had gone on. "Care for a bowl of Cheerios?" I said, and Martha said, "Sure," and sat down with her daughter at the table.

CHRISTMAS IN QUEENS

THIS MORNING I made Ramen noodles with extra veggies in it, and peanut butter and Korean bean paste. Then I took a walk, crossed Grand Central on over to Queens Boulevard where an Asian woman walking a little dog caught my eye. She saw my eye was caught by her, so when she got up close, I said "Hmmph" as I sometimes do to Asian women walking little dogs, not to turn my nose up at her, gee wiz, no, not ever, but to open a window. Though I smiled, she did not appreciate the sound I had made. So I walked on through Forest Hills.

While circling back through the neighborhood, a little trash pile between the sidewalk and street caught my eye. It was just a pile of sticks and twigs, pretty much, but right there on top, quite clearly thrown away on purpose, and covered with dust, was a ten-dollar bill folded in half. I lifted it, unfolded it, saw the five-dollar bill enclosed within it, looked around to see was anybody observing me, then pulled out my wallet, inserted the money, and walked on, thinking maybe someone didn't want that money because the person it had belonged to died or something.

I didn't know, but it was a decent gift. I was fifteen dollars richer, and much richer still for what the Asian gave me, the "hmmph," the only word I have spoken today.

2 SLAPS

I SLAPPED Chelsea in the video store, but it's not what you think. I slapped my Chelsea over this girl who like slapped me all so long ago in my room, when I lived on the south side. And when she slapped me, that girl, I felt so awesome, so like I mattered, so like somebody loved me. Before then, the only slaps I'd had were unfriendly ones, slaps slapped in anger, like the times my mother slapped me, or the time I got bitch-slapped in the school parking lot by a jock, and the people standing around laughed. When the girl I was in love with slapped me, I felt warm and alive, like the greatest thing ever. This may well have been the happiest, most contented, meaningful moment of my life.

When I slapped Chelsea across the face in the video store, though, she did not feel like the greatest thing ever. The way Chelsea acted, jerking her head back and looking at me with that face, I felt uncomfortable. Chelsea acted like I had just assaulted her.

We rented the movie anyway, and went home, where we lived in the heart of the town, and watched it. It was called *Trust* by Hal Hartley. The main guy in the movie tells the main woman in the movie that respect and admiration are better than love because when people are in love they do stupid shit, like commit suicide.

The next day Chelsea says to me, "I realized last night that I need to make a decision."

"I said I was sorry."

"No, you don't realize what is going on here. That thing you did was totally unacceptable."

"I'm sorry, Chelsea, it just felt right is all. I know how it sounds, that I say I slapped you because I love you, but it's true, and I didn't slap you very hard, either, did I?"

"See, you don't even care. You're still making excuses for it."

"What am I supposed to say?"

"I need to see that you are self-aware enough to know that you are a violent person who is dangerous. What if a year down the road you start beating me black and blue and giving me shiners and totally shredding me to pieces to where I keep going to the woman's shelter only to run home to you and have you slap me around all over again?"

"But that could never possibly in a million years happen and you know it."

"Oh really? How do I know it? You did it once. Who's to say you won't do it again?"

"I just would never do that. You know me better."

We married later that year, and I never slapped her again, not once during all the time we were together, about eight years. The things we needed but could not get from each other we sought elsewhere, on the sly, on other young human beings electrified by sex and the desire to be noticed. I released aggression on a zinester who wanted me to choke her, and she, my wife, found her desired tenderness in a construction worker. We suffered. We cried. The agony of our breakup was the same agony I felt when the girl who slapped me dumped me for a college girl. And so: the guy in Hal Hartley's movie could be right. Respect and admiration are better than love. All I know is that when I slapped Chelsea in the video store, the feeling that made me do it came from a place of joy. When she looked up from the rack of movies, where she was browsing, and smiled, my love bubbled up and I slapped her. Is that really so hard to understand?

DORM

CHOCHI RESTLESS. In her room. All day. In her room. All her thing everywhere. It weird. It close. Chochi alone. Chochi walk down the stair. Chochi hard shoe click. Chochi pass kitchen. Voices of girls. Plates clink, silverware. A red exit sign and Chochi push. The lever. Walk outside. It fresh. Snowing. Chochi walk down. A hill. To a lake. Freezing. Ice in the water. Smoke a cigarette. Walk back up. To her room. She on the bed, sitting. Hands in her lap. Looking up at Chochi meanly.

"What?" Chochi say.

"I heard your feet coming down the stairs."

"And?"

"You walked right by where I was working without coming in to say hello."

"I didn't know you were in there. How was I to know?"

"You could have checked."

"All those girls make me nervous."

"You walked by and didn't come in to kiss me while I was washing the dishes. It would have meant so much."

"I'm sorry."

She look from Chochi. To the floor. Shake her head. Bring a hand up to scratch the back of her neck, and Chochi thinking *I'm such a moron.*

Now she look up at Chochi, happy. As if all the shaking her head at the floor was only her. Making up her mind. And she has decided, yes, Chochi see it in her face—love! She stand up and wrap Chochi in her arms.

Chochi kiss her fat lips, her. Lips that melt Chochi, make Chochi weaker than Chochi is. More stupid. More not caring so Chochi fuck her in. Heap of dirty clothes against wall, her. Body is brown, she. Say she and Chochi need to go to Karen's tonight.

"Karen's?"

"Don't make fun of my friends."

"I'm not," Chochi say. "I'd Love to go to Karen's."

"No you wouldn't," she say. "That's what we were supposed to do last night, but we didn't."

"I liked what we did better," Chochi say.

"How do you even know?" she say. "We didn't go there because you were too afraid of being around other people and letting them know how much you love me."

"What?"

"You heard me."

"I love being around other people," Chochi say. "I thought, being I only had a few days, we could spend it together."

"We'll go tonight," she say.

"Sure," Chochi say.

But Chochi fuck her in. Again. Until after midnight. Chochi look out the window. At the falling snow and tell her a thousand miles away, in the place from where

Chochi drove, it all sunshine.

But that not true. Florida the same time zone. Stupid Chochi.

She talk Chochi into putting. On clothes. Go out for air. So Chochi. Go down with her, holding hand. Chochi walk. Along the pretty brick path in the wonderland. Campus of brick. Buildings. Chochi. And she come up. On a soccer field. Girls. Are here from the same building—R—that she is from. She go to them. Talk to them. Introduce Chochi, the man.

The girls. With short, close hair, like high school football players, ignore Chochi, even at her imploring. She want to show Chochi. Off, she. Bragging, *Hey, look here, he drove a thousand miles to fuck me. I'm getting fucked all I like. Yeah.* But these girls are not. Interested. Their ears are red. They slide down the bank on cookie tins and sleds. Chochi figure. Chochi will be funny, and run, jump onto the bank on stomach, slide down it the way Frosty. The Snowman do when he look for a warm. Spot for the little girl who is cold.

Chochi. Don't get no congrats. The girls. Hiss at Chochi like snakes, look at Chochi mean with dripping teeth. And stuff. "Don't do that," they say. "You want to ruin the bank for the rest of us? Look what you did."

The girl Chochi love, she. Look at Chochi, her face beside the other faces, her face a face of the other faces.

Chochi has made a fool of Chochi. Self, Chochi know it. "How was I to know the snow would fall apart like that?" Chochi tell her.

She smile. At Chochi. With a look say, *No, hey, it's okay, don't worry about them. You are way more important.*

And Chochi think. A flash. Of what she say Chochi in a letter: "I don't feel right wearing dresses anymore." Chochi think: "Who would?" But it nothing Chochi. Ever say to her. Instead Chochi take. Her great fat small. Hand, and Chochi and she walk into the soccer field to roll a snowy man. Chochi and she roll up snowy balls while the other girls laugh and have so much fun. Sliding down the bank of snow. And the girl Chochi love. She on purpose don't look at them. Ignore them. So that. Maybe. They will look at her, with her man, her Chochi dick, and think, *Wow, check her out*. But they do not. In this world the only thing a Chochi dick good for is cutting. Off—throw it into a fire somewhere to help a bum warm his hands.

Chochi build. Chochi snowy man. With she. Chochi stick pennies into his face for eyes and a mouth. He look sick. Like a sick snowy man, like he got disease. Anybody looking at him will think it. So Chochi. And she turn away from it, both with shame holding. Hands, feeling the cold snowy wetness of each other's palms. And climb. The bank. Together and walk on the brick path, the other girls walking happily in front of Chochi and she, Chochi. Feel his love wish it was she and them, not she and Chochi. Chochi useless. Dresses are evil. Chochi ruin her. Image. Chochi make her. Into something vile in the eyes. Of her friends. It make Chochi. *Feel*—because Chochi *love* her— *oh*—rotted, a. Burden hampering her better progression.

Chochi and. She follow the girls. Back to the dorm. Go inside, into the warm girlsmelling air. Of perfect waxed floor. Climb the stair. Up to the love den. Chochi losing Chochi popularity with her. Chochi feel it. Seeping away in the crack under the door. It not how she wanted it to be, it. Not why she sent Chochi her BP card, why Chochi drove a thousand mile to see her, Chochi.

Would drove ten. Thousand. Mile. If to be with her a minute, and.

Ten. Thousand. More Chochi would drive. A billion because. Chochi. *Love* her. With Chochi love there are no mile, no light year.

Chochi put. Chochi hand on her. It losing. It backbone. She does. Not make the sound when she see Chochi naked now. Lust does. Not sparkle. In her eye. Perhaps she thinking of the girls? She do not speak out loud for Chochi to fuck her now, but. It all Chochi have. So Chochi fuck her in her. Bed and Chochi know. She do. Not want it, Chochi.

Think, *She never cared. She used me. I horrified her friends. Cut it off! Throw it in the fire!*

In the morning while she sleep Chochi. Look out the window at the snowy place. Big women in jackets with college name on their backs cart in food. For the kitchen downstairs. The food, Chochi think, will feed girls. Chochi see. Girl mouths. Many many, dozens, open. Let in forks for food, Chochi. Look at Chochi love On her stomach, her shaved calves uncovered, her feet. Hanging over the edge of the bed. And Chochi. Know. How far Chochi will drive. To get back, the. Thought pain Chochi. To be away from her, and what they say in Sociology 101? It take five friends. To do a thing. Then you do it too, he.

Looking at her calves. Like that. Uncovered along the bed, the light coming in that Chochi hate now, wishing the light was gone. There is little Chochi can do to help. Chochi self. Chochi start with her feet, he.

Lick them. Lick her ankles, lick her knees. Lick and lick but oh, she do. Not want him, even. When his tongue is.

The door knock.

"I want you to leave," she say, and Chochi go, a day. Earlier from the plan, she hold. Nothing against Chochi, but Chochi know. New plan is. Stop. Sever. Forget. Chochi.

Drive a thousand mile straight, use her BP card for gas, for coffee—*would she be happy to see me drinking coffee?—see me being safe?—keeping myself alive?*—No!

Chochi write her but she no, don't. Write back, she. Don't care, don't care, she don't. Write Chochi for many letters, and. Then a letter from her arrive, oh, Chochi kiss it and kiss it, kiss it and kiss it and oh! *My darling*, Chochi think, *my. Darling* before he even open the letter, *my darling* and, this love, it. Awful, it horrible, it terrible, awful, but Chochi open the. Letter and. Read that she has a girl. Friend, don't hold this against me, Chochi *die, die!* Oh, it hurt, it hurt and Chochi hate Chochi, Chochi stupid, Chochi remember her when she. Look at him when he. Drip sweat on her and he. Lick her and fuck her in her dorm and the door knock and he fuck down on her, she. Struggle, but Chochi fuck her till she bite him and then Chochi let her go and she put on dress and open door for inspectors of the dorm, they. See Chochi under covers, and she blush and they look. At her. They smell it. They know, they. Giggle, and say the paint on the walls are fine, and. When they gone Chochi fuck her in her.

Oh, she look up at Chochi with. Eyes, her. Body Chochi will miss for the rest of his life, her. Eyes he will remember and her smell and his tongue in her and she destroys him, she. Has murdered Chochi, Chochi will. Miss her forever and will never leave that room, that moment, that box, that view of her from the sky, that. Open sore will grow. Will cover Chochi and suffocate him.

THESE KIDS WERE THE CHOSEN ONES

BROWN FUMED on the rock while Pink looked pissed. And Yellow. They saw not why Brown was denied. They thought Brown should eat too, that he was our hero despite what I said, that you don't go jeopardize a trip for cheap heroics, which is exactly what happened earlier when he pulled a halibut into the canoe. A stunt like that could ruin the whole trip. Brown had acted like he understood, but why then was he over there being the martyr? It was bad for morale, having Brown pout around that way. I needed the colors to know. On this issue I could not let Brown slide.

After dinner I asked Alfredo, on the payroll this year as chaperone, what he thought of my decision. We were on a log, staring across Waydelich Cove at the Oliver Glacier, and Alfredo cleared his throat. "I am no doctor, like you, sir, but I have seven children. When you pick out one to use as the sample, sometimes the others make more troubles."

"More trouble?"

"Yes sir."

"Can you give me an example, Alfredo?"

"Yes sir. You know Carlita?"

"Sure, I've met all your children."

"I one time grounded her for a week."

"Why'd you do that?"

"I did not want her being, you know, a loose."

"A loose?"

"Yes sir. I had a feeling Carlita was becoming a too loose, you know, how she would dress up and look at herself in the glass? I did not want her, you know, to be a loose."

"And so you grounded her."

"Yes, but the others sneaked food for her and they acted up. Manuel broke Consuela's mandolin so I had to punish him too. It became a competition of who could be baddest and so before long I had to punish everybody. It was a terrible. I felt like a dog."

"I see," I said, and bummed another smoke from Alfredo. We watched the light crawl through Oliver's fissures in aquamarine flashes and crimson and yellow. It was a beautiful summer night and the fine display would last until about midnight when things dimmed and the evergreens held themselves close. It was an amusing story, but I saw no parallel here. These were delinquent juveniles who knew what a privilege it was to be part of the Wilderness Program. These kids were hand selected. These kids were chosen.

For breakfast we ate halibut tortillas with scrambled eggs mixed in. I had lifted the ban on Brown, so it was a new day. The morale was good. We packed up the tents and loaded the canoes and pushed back out for another day on the waters. We rode up close to the Oliver Glacier, paddling around icebergs carefully and at plenty of distance. Sometimes an iceberg will split and roll over without warning. It's a tricky business canoeing through icebergs.

Oh, but the beauty we experienced, what a sight! Brown, Black and Blue and Yellow and all of the other colors went ooh and ahh.

We paddled alongside the coast then across the channel to Charmers Island to see the bears. It took all day to get there, and there were lots of complaints of sore muscles. I told the colors that pain was part of the program. The colors were here to find themselves, not whimper and whine. They knew it, yet still spoke lustily of civilization's charms, of hamburgers from McDonald's and hot water. Yellow even waxed rhapsodic over doughnuts. "Where's your adventuresome spirit?" I said. "This island has tons of bears on it. Don't you want to see some bears?"

"No, I hate bears, bears are stupid!" Red cried. Red's file contained a tidbit about this thing she had done to her smaller brother. It's confidential, but you can be sure I felt sorry for her parents. How awful it must've been to have Red as your daughter.

"Red," I said. "You shouldn't raise your voice at me."

"Why not? This wasn't my idea! I didn't want to come out here! I hate the goddamn wilderness! I've always hated it!"

"Watch your mouth, Red," Alfredo said.

Brown said, "Stop whining, Red."

Thank you, I thought, and gave him the nod of respect.

"Yeah," Blue said. "How can we find ourselves if you are always complaining?"

"OK, let's calm down here," I said, and we voted. The adventuresome spirit won out over the sorry naysayers and we went to find some bears. We cut into the forest on up to a broad muskeg, a delight to behold. I thought we were making real progress, but then I look back and Brown and Red are gone. "Alfredo, what happened to Brown and Red?"

Alfredo raised his shoulders with a look.

"Goddamnit Alfredo, you were supposed to watch them."

"Red is a too loose," Alfredo said.

"Come again?"

"You tell us to learn from our mistakes," Alfredo said, repeating the gist of one of my lectures. "When a girl is too loose, if you try to make her tight, she become a more loose."

"What's this got to do with anything, Alfredo!" I nearly yelled.

There were snickers from the colors. They were laughing at me.

"If you wanting to run a tight ship, sometime you have to be not so controlling. I guess they made a run for it when I was not looking."

"OK, everybody, back to the camp," I said.

Hems and haws commenced, but what was I to do? In ten years of wildernessing I'd never lost a color. When we got to camp, sure enough, a canoe was gone. Brown and Red were far out in the water, the stupid sons of bitches. What did they think? That they would make it back to civilization? They were dead ducks and I was in no mood to be a hero today. I bummed a smoke from Alfredo and sat on a log. I exhaled through my nose and thought of punishments both cruel and unusual. Yes, it was my job to go after them. If I didn't, Mother Nature would swallow Brown and Red like jujubes. I would be accused of steering a loose ship. When my cigarette ended, I deputized Black and Blue, and the three of us, with provisions and plenty of rope to tie those bastards up with, pushed out after them into the water.

RIVER JOKES

IT WAS THE FAILING of the light, but mostly it was the scratchy trees. The farther she went, the more scratchy trees there were until she could not move without getting scratched by the scratchy trees. When the twigs of the scratchy trees came together so that it was no longer a bunch of small scratchy trees, but more like one very long scratchy tree, she crouched down to the ground where the twigs were less, and crawled there, beneath it, through tunnels and throughways other animals used for passage.

The scratchy trees released her into a clearing where a dead oak, its upper half broken and leaning, prevented the small scratchy trees from growing. She was happy to stand, but wanted her shoes. She would give anything for her shoes. She would be good, be cheerful and love her daddies. She would be good forever if somewhere in this clearing her shoes just happened to be there. She would do anything for her shoes.

She looked at her hand to see how good she could see

in how dark it was getting. Then she looked around trying to think of which way the road was. Couldn't be far. Roads were everywhere in the world. All you had to do was keep going and you'd find the road.

She sat on a log to get a good scratch at her mosquito bites. There was another tree, a branchless rotted thing coming up from the ground a few steps away. As she scratched her bites she looked at the tree. It looked like she could push it down if she wanted. She got up and grabbed it and pushed on it and the tree crackled and leaned, its roots breaking the ground at her feet and the yellow jackets flowering up.

She had never been stung, not by one of those. She had never seen a yellow jacket before, and the first one, having stung her wrist, made her scream, and she slapped it, killing it, but the sting kept stinging, and before she could think about how much it hurt, and coddle it, feeling sorry for herself, another sting stung. The stinging bees were on her knees, on her back, on her face, between her toes, all of them stinging, buzzing, swarming around her so that she had no choice but to run into the scratchy trees whose thorns pierced her skin, drawing blood as the retractable needles of the yellow jackets went in, and pulled out, time and again like so many little sewing machines.

***

Her fat daddy was on the moss, the soft green patch of it upon which they'd eaten dinner. Her skinny daddy was beside him. Together they sat in the French bathing suits, their legs, the skinny ones and the fat ones, all four, moving down the slope of moss and pointing at the river, their twenty toes in a position to be counted, one through twenty. Her fat daddy said, "Did I ever tell you, Hank, how the Wassissa River got its name?"

Her daddies had watched the sun set over the river. Now they were enjoying the stars, which were all so pretty up there, the way they twinkled. The Big Dipper hovered above the trees, having lifted out a nice fresh drink.

"How?" her skinny daddy said.

"Well," her fat daddy said. He slapped a mosquito on his belly. He took a deep breath of air and let it out slowly. "A long time ago," he said, "these two black fellers were walking through the woods, minding their own business. They came across the water here that we are looking at now, and the first one says, *Wass iss?*"

"I love it," her skinny daddy said.

"But I haven't finished," her fat daddy said. "Don't you want to know what the second fellow said?"

"Oh please," her skinny daddy said. "Spare me the agony."

HORSE'S DAD, UHM

WE TALKED ALONG on backs, told stories on people we'd known who'd hurt theirs. In the telling of our back stories we drank Lowenbrau in bottles. In no time we were drunk and Horse went in about his dad who'd been in "Nam." Horse narrated the jungle skirmish during which time his dad stepped on a landmine. He said, "My dad was blown in two."

I laughed. Oh Jesus, his dad getting all blown in two and all. My eyes roved around the room, searched out something to help me stop laughing, to pass my laughter off on. The horses, Jesus. Horse had all these like cheap ceramic horse statue things you see people selling roadside. He'd decorated his apartment with them, had a horse lampshade, posters of horses on the walls, on his coffee table a dead horse ashtray. You rested your cigarette between two ribs.

I pointed to a glittery rearing horse, pretending like my laughter was over it, adding insult to injury, judging by the look of deepening horror on Horse's face, his face that is kind of like a horse's face. It's kind of long like a horse's face, see? Horse's face, though, has nothing to do with why Horse is called Horse.

Horse is called Horse over the what he pulls out when challenged. I know. Once, not long after Mary and I moved in, Horse drove me in his El Camino to a bar in a sleazy part of Saint Pete. While there, the subject of his name came up. Horse stuck his boot on a barstool rung, raised up and whipped it out. He plopped it onto the lacquered bar top where it writhed like a serpent or snake, whatever's the difference. He dumped beer on it and the thing splashed around, growing, straightening out in the puddle of beer. "Put that thang away!" the female bartender screamed, and Horse honored the request.

I was laughing. The two halves of Horse's dad, right? The upper half that included his back and belly and head and arms I saw over in one part of the jungle, and the lower half that would have been his legs and butt and member in another. Each time I tried to stop laughing, Jesus, it just looked like I was trying to hide my merriment over what had happened to Horse's dad. When I looked at Horse and saw his stricken face, the words that came to me were, "Is he still alive?"

"Man," Horse said, "he was blown in two, I told you that!"

"Yeah," I said, "but I was thinking they might have saved the good half."

"He's dead! My own father!"

"I'm sorry," I said, sniggering and snickering, trying to hold it in, but guffawing, Jesus. "I can't help this!" I yelled, snot coming out of my nose and all. "I don't know why I'm laughing!" I cried, and pictured it more and laughed more and told myself there was nothing funny about any of this, goddamnit, but I kept on laughing, everybody else in the room quiet but for me, looking at me sadly, disgustedly, this was going too far, and Steve from Hawaii—pronounced with a V, Ha*v*aii, in case you didn't know—up and left us, as did Nicole who swears to God she is pregnant with the mayor's baby. They left me to make a fool and a jerk of myself in front of Horse and Mary Wheeler, my sweetie. They made no effort to save me from humiliation, from disgrace.

I could not, I tell you, stop laughing, even when Horse began to shake, his body jerking as he thought of his poor dad's two halves thrown separate ways across the jungle floor. As I laughed on, Horse began to weep. The jerking of Horse's body aggravated his back pain. He reached around, grimacing. Poor Horse had hurt his back when he fell through the ice-cream factory floor in Clearwater— he'd been toting a hundred-pound bag of sugar at the time. Since then we on the upper floor—Steve and Nicole and Mary Wheeler and I—had not been receiving our free weekly packages of Klondike Bars.

"I'm sorry this happened," Mary said, and pulled me out of Horse's place back onto the balcony of the Spanish Villa, pulled me back to ours where my laughter disappeared like a bubble you see floating through the sunshine in a park. Now you see it, now you don't. "What the hell was that about?" my Mary wanted to know, and I saw Horse's dad blown in two in my mind again. It wasn't funny, but I had just finished reading, again, of the adventures of David in the *Book of Samuel*, where in exchange for the king's daughter David kills two hundred dudes and cuts off their foreskins. Am I trying to pass my laughter off on the king's daughter, the story where David dumps out his bag of foreskins onto a table so that they can be counted? Probably, but who's to say for sure? Not everything in the world makes sense, does it?

Take me. All day every day I'm like on the balcony reading the bible in shorts, shirtless with my bare feet on the rail. I am living off my insurance settlement. All I did was break my jaw in the crash, and dislocate my foot, nothing big. Didn't hurt my back. I just sit here day after day reading the King James Version, watching the palm tree fruit change color. I watch the fruit turn from green to yellow to orange, then fall to the ground where it begins to rot.

POSSUM

HE DOESN'T EAT. He's lost twenty pounds. When he doesn't show for class, will somebody come to the house, knock, feel worried? His car will be parked outside, so what is this? And what's that smell? When the summer began, a possum crawled under the house and died. When the smell first hit them, he was too distraught to mention it, and neither did she. They were not speaking. Flies attacked the house. They left it under there for two weeks before he called somebody to fish it out. It was the size of a dog, the guy said, and with a tiny sly smile said, "Rigor mortis has set in." She made secret plans. By the end of summer she left him for a guy she reconnected with on Facebook, and he was no longer hungry.

GIFTS OF THE TORNADO

MY BROTHER flew to Sydney to study the mating habits of red kangaroos. Before leaving, he said, "Come live at my place in Queens while I'm gone," so I did that. I was in his kitchen, a newly divorced king, when the world outside his window exploded with hailstones and crazy rains. Ripped shrubs flew by and trashcans and the plastic toys of children. The havoc ended a minute later, and I walked through the neighborhood where oak trees had held fast for a hundred years. Now they were toppled, the sidewalks upended. Kids in yarmulkes and tassels were down in the holes where the roots had been, playing games. Crunching through shiny nuggets of broken tempered glass along Jewel Avenue, I made it to the liquor store whose owner stood out front with crossed arms thick and hairy. He said, "Unbelievable."

"Yeah, crazy, right?"

"God is angry," he said, and said, "Look at this." He pointed to a Mercedes-Benz. Limbs had fallen around it in a perfect rectangle, not a leaf on it while cars and vans up and down Jewel Avenue looked to have been stomped on by Godzilla.

Just then a woman in a pink hoody stepped up from the street and asked a fellow straddling a bicycle if she could use his phone. The woman wore green flipflops and loose jeans with holes in the knees.

"Are you open for business?" I asked the liquor salesman.

"Go in, take what you want, but hurry. If my wife don't forgive me, then I don't know."

"Your wife?" I wanted to know more, like what did he do to need forgiveness, but he gave me a look that said *Don't try it*, so I went in and grabbed something clear and cheap. Back on the sidewalk, I said, "How much?"

"No more!" he shouted.

"Okay, I'll pay you later."

The woman in the pink hoodie still was trying to borrow a phone, and she looked frazzled, like she had been though a great trial and was in shock. "I need to get home to my children," she explained to a couple in their car, their hazard lights flashing. She was Hispanic. A few curled locks bobbed down over her forehead.

I wanted to help, but I didn't have my phone with me. I wanted to take her home, she with her baggy clothes hanging all over her thin body. She looked malnourished. I was about to be brave, be bold, be extroverted, walk over there and say she could use my phone at my place two blocks down. I had already put the plan into motion, only an arm reached out from the car window with a phone. She took it and pressed in some numbers and held the phone to her ear. Somebody answered. Whoever was on the other end, I wanted to be that person.

Returning to the apartment through the devastation, a horror movie here with sirens and faraway screams and gridlocked traffic, I thought of my brother in Australia. Before setting out on his grand adventure, he said kangaroos have three vaginas. The vaginas on the sides are for intercourse while the vagina in the middle is for delivering the joey. Sometimes roos have as many as three joeys, my brother said, each joey the size of a jellybean. I thought of this while walking past Hasidic families standing in their courtyards discussing the damage. Wherever I looked, people were weirded out. People stumbled along like zombies, as if they had emerged from the holes, those dark portals to the underworld ripped free by trees.

Once in my brother's apartment, I took the beans off simmer, enough beans here for a family of five. Using a coffee cup, I scooped out a serving and filled a bowl. I ate on the foldout bed. The three vaginas seemed related to why I was here, for wasn't it after the second one that she left me? Along with her that made three.

I started in on the vodka, blacked out. Come dawn I rose. I looked through the window at the world. Nobody had repaired things during the night, but I heard chainsaws, people working together, rebuilding. I wanted to call my wife, wanted to tell her of the tornado but then I remembered—she wasn't my wife anymore. When I heard later that only one person died from the falling trees, just some nun who'd been parked in her car two blocks down, I felt a deep pang of jealousy. I felt as though I had been cheated.

MELT

I ATE IT in the big room of the shack whose porch I cut her up on, cutting her into pieces that dropped into the can. Did I eat it on the couch while watching some televangelist evangelize on the small black and white? I watched a lot of that then. Robert Tilton, you know? Benny Hinn and Jack Van Impe. *Forgive me, Father, for I have sinned!* Though I do not remember eating it, how I cut her up into tiny pieces I remember clear and crisp. I see her pieces falling. That was in Florida.

Twenty years later I dismember another woman, this time with bare hands, ripping her apart in Kew Gardens Hills, my crime followed by a long walk along Main Street into Flushing. Don't you love that word? I love it. Don't get flushed in Flushing, y'all!

I felt nobody should see her that way is why, each rip parcel to the puzzle that should you be so lucky as to have *all* of the ripped pieces, you might unrip her. Like they did with the Six Million Dollar Man, you could fit her back together—here's your Six Million Dollar Woman done up special in pigmented safflower oil. When somebody does that to gelatin silver, you know they care about the person in the picture. It takes patience. And love.

So I crumple a rip up of her here and there and toss it. There's her foot on the concrete fronting the Jewish bakery. Should anybody stoop to pick it up, what will they think? I think they will think *Somebody ripped this*, and tell by the size of the piece, and size of the foot within the ripped piece, the rough dimensions of the rectangle from which it was ripped.

Sixteen by twenty.

Into the strip of grass alongside the Jewish graveyard I toss her vagina, leaving a trail, you know? Foot, vagina, rip of a mouth, a ripped aureole. Check out her burnished-looking knee right there while beyond the chain-link fence the markers have stones on them like in *Schindler's List*, how at the end of the movie you see the progeny of the people Schindler saved putting stones on his grave to say how grateful they are. Whenever I walk by this graveyard, I think of Liam Neeson, who played Schindler, of the wild privileges of the Nazi officials, and suffering women.

I said I tossed out her vagina, but in truth I ripped it into three pieces, putting difficulty into the whole thing should somebody pick her pieces off the ground while walking happily up and down Main Street. It's what I would do. I pick stuff up all the time. If I were me, I would pick up the bottom half of her vagina then search for the other pieces. I would take the pieces home with me. If I were me, I would piece her back together, and in this way save her.

***

I squirted kerosene into the can the meat part came out of then struck a match and dropped it in there. Flames rose. Black smoke clouded the porch, the tiny pieces curling up, melting, but the fire died, leaving many shriveled parts of her in the stink of scorched acetate. My attempt at absolution through burning wasn't working. Forces worked against me. In haste I pinched a piece up and held it to the light while looking through my loupe. There was my organ in her, not all the way, but half. If I pieced the surviving pieces together, uncutting her, I could see her flat on her back again, on the blanket with arms and legs and feet thrown up and the gun in her gut, for I had fitted her, you see, the whole of her into the vertical frame. My Zeiss Ikon took her *all* the way in, knees and thighs and shins a gloriously shining capital M. She had trusted me. "Don't do anything illegal," she even said, but was of age now. It was wrong, what I had done, and was doing, this destruction of the record. Destroying her, I knew I was destroying myself.

***

Her last piece is an eye shaped like an almond, its iris painted blue in imitation of the real eyes whose Asian tilt paired with its Aryan tint always turned me on. Simply put, she is hotter than a pair of jumper cables at a Willkillya County family reunion. If you don't know what Willkillya County is, it's the pet name for Wakulla County, Florida, what people who live there call it, and where parts of the *Creature from the Black Lagoon* were filmed. Her people are from Pinellas County where they have labored in strawberries for generations. Her desire to not be a part of that earthy crew of yore, here in her advanced education, creativity and sophistication, compels me. But whenever I went to Willkillya to party with my friends, she stayed behind. She did not like hanging out with rednecks.

She is the one I watched *Schindler's List* with, a movie we enjoyed for a dollar each at Movies 8 in Leon County. She is not interested in her ancestry other than where it concerns her grandmother, who had loved her more, she always said, than her mom, and who walked into the gulf one night never to return. It's a thing we have in common, she and I, that our grandmothers both committed suicide.

Her eyes I leave on the walks of Flushing.

On the walks of Flushing her eyes I leave.

Then I am in the neutral stretch of ground, the no-man's land between Israel and Asia, as it were, retracing and seeing, as I regress, the pieces of my life now on the ground, each a stone of gratitude—*thank you, thank you for having loved me!* Passing a rip of breast on the steps of John Browne High School, I don't even slow. I pass a hand with a ring on it tossed to the side of a hair salon. I pass her parts but do not stoop down, not for the mouth of the loveliest lips God ever made, or the rip that cradles her clitoris.

When she left, I felt like a tossed out old shoe with holes in it, dirty laces haywire and frayed, nothing you'd go back for, nothing a reasonable person would try and save.

Yet the next day, waking, I'm like, *Oh shit, what if somebody walking along Main Street starts picking my rips up and unripping her?*

In a panic I dress. Don't do coffee, just leave and head up Jewel Avenue and hook north, searching for what I left behind. I find this and that, this over here and that over there, an elbow by the Jewish laundromat, a few rips of nothing and some cheekbone by the kosher deli garbage can. These rips I carry home with me. I put them on the floor and try re-piecing things. I want to repair what's been broken but nothing fits. All I have is a monster.

THE GIRL IN THE GUTTER

HALFWAY DOWN the hill a drop of rain hits your face. A step later the sky pops like a water balloon and you duck under the awning of a Shoe Rack. That's when you see the girl in the gutter and slip out your Canon, hit the button. The screen lights up. You zero in on her, take a picture, but she stands. Then falls. Again she is in the gutter rushing already heavily with water. Before you can pocket your camera and maybe like help out or something, a salaryman appears. You move back farther into the shadows.

Cars fly by this way and that way, splashing through puddles as the salaryman tugs at the girl in the white sleeveless dress. He tugs her out of the gutter onto the sidewalk. She is making progress. He gets her on her feet but lets go and she drops back onto the concrete. The guy walks over to the International Money Exchange next to where you are kicked back under the overhang. You watch him unzip his slacks. He starts pissing on the glass door.

That's when you see the umbrella, oh, a small ladies' model. She'd been caught in the rain, as happens, only was too sauced up to open it before getting drenched. Now she crawls with her closed umbrella clutched in one hand, knuckles scraping the sidewalk, the black purse looped over her neck hanging down like a cow bell. When she reaches the thin city tree, she lets go of the umbrella and grabs hold of the tree, trying to get back onto her feet.

The rain and wind have lightened yet she appears to be fighting a hurricane, her body contorting into weird, half-collapsed positions that remind you of Picasso's abstract portraits. Again she falls, her face on the grate now at the base of the tree, her butt in the air. You have fallen into a trance watching her under the awning where all is dry and warm. It is a movie. A plot here unfolds. You want to find out what's next so watch on eagerly as she rises to her knees and sticks fingers down her throat— looks like her whole hand is entering her mouth—trying to vomit. You snap off a shot.

The salaryman finishes peeing on the door of the International Money Exchange. He returns to her and helps her stand, but again she grabs onto the skinny tree, claws it, clutching it, face thrown back against the streetlamp and falling rain, tiny mouth puckered and smiling. The salaryman, still trying to help, grabs hold of her dress. She slips down the skinny tree, the dress rising higher along her body as she slips, her underwear and belly now exposed. People walking by on the sidewalk with opened umbrellas pause now and then, take note of her, and walk on. The salaryman lets go. She falls onto her back, her legs fly up. You consider your responsibilities as an alienated non-citizen of the locale. Is the salaryman her friend, or did he, as did you, stumble across her as the rain began? You do not see what good it will do to interfere, so hit her once more with your Canon.

The salaryman looks to traffic. He is trying to hail a cab, but the cabs are not stopping. He grabs the girl's hand. He pulls her into a sitting position. Her energy has waned. Is she going down? The guy jostles her as she sits on her butt on the concrete, legs wide open to the cars that appear to drive straight up her skirt. The repetitive motion makes you think of colonial conquest and the mistreatment of Korea by countries such as Japan, China, the United States. And guys like you—*Westerners* you are called. The Yongsan Garrison is only right up the street.

Such go your thoughts while watching the attractive young woman, the *aggassi*, get pounded by rain.

Once more she is on her feet. The salaryman herds her into the street where they both reach out to cabs. Several taxis crawl to a stop as if to give the couple a lift, but speed onward at the realization that this girl could vomit. Who is gonna clean that up? Knowledgeable on vomiting young women, the drivers drive on. One peels out while the girl holds onto the door handle. On rickety giraffe legs she nearly falls again, but her date, if he is her date, catches her. A bus nearly plows them both over.

This goes on for a bit, you taking pictures until a cab finally pulls over for them.

Then they are gone, but this is the *jangma*, the year's first outbreak of the Korean rainy season. You've been caught with no umbrella in a rain Koreans say is radioactive. The rain falls on your head, you go bald to bed. Though scientific evidence refutes this, Koreans persist in the belief due to that little mishap over there in

Japan, the notorious *Fukushima* nuclear fiasco. That's why Koreans carry umbrellas every day, rain or shine.

This rain may not stop for days. You'll soak yourself getting back to the place you rest your head. Lucky for you, the girl has left you her umbrella with the clear panels. You run over there and grab it and run it back to your safe place under the awning of the Shoe Rack. You pop off the strap. You pop it open and use it to get back home. In this way, you have profited from a young Korean woman's misfortune.

HAPPY SHORTEST DAY OF THE YEAR, 2025

MY MOTHER says she beat me with an umbrella.

"Oh really?"

"It was in Aix-en-Provence, when you were about 5 years old."

She is 84 now, and I am 58. I am on my back on the foldout couch in her spare room at a retirement community in Florida. It is early in the morning. I drove here yesterday and the day before from New Jersey.

"We were driving," she says, "and you started screaming in the car about a bee. You wouldn't calm down so your father told me to beat you with it. I guess I did what he said but this made things worse. You went into an asthmatic fit and we weren't sure if we should take you to a hospital."

The memory plays out. First it was the bee, and then, while that trauma still was going on, to see my mother coming at me with an umbrella, to beat me with it, and then actually beating me with it, it drove me into a catatonic state.

I ask if I could have been putting on an act, as kids do. "No, no, there was no way," she says, and thinks out loud about how it felt so wrong to do such a thing. "I was basically your father's slave," she says, and mentions the times that my father, too, performed violence on me when I was a small boy. He had belted me, he had belted my little brother, he had choked me, he had slammed a bag of potatoes over my head, had made me take my clothes off, stuff like that.

I don't consider it anything worth complaining about, for these are my treasures.

But the umbrella, this is the first I've heard of the umbrella.

On the shortest day of the year.

BLACK VOMIT

FIVE HOURS—that's what he had to kill before his plane left Vancouver for LaGuardia, and already he felt dismayed to hear English. It grossed him out. And the ugliness, the stupid facial hair variations of the men, the droopy jeans on them, on the young and old alike. Women blowing noses. Old men pointing canes. Fat drooping butts, fat drooping boobs, the men strappy in sandals, going for athletic looks, their feet red and yellow and crusty and swollen with nasty toenails. The Reeboks and Nikes, the New Balance. He felt sick. Needed to do a number two in the bathroom.

Bathrooms were all over the airport, but whenever he went in one white devils, just the most godawful apparitions, were busy with their business. They *shalumphed* into the toilet while pulling pricks out. Was he to do same? He found another but this one was no better. Here too ugly red-faced dudes in running shoes or man sandals whipped their schlongs out while walking to the stalls. He went bathroom to bathroom, and round again, hoping to catch a snatch of privacy.

Between bathrooms one guy let out an exuberant screeching whistle to catch his buddy's attention twenty yards off. The red-faced guy's teeth were in the open, framed by the long up-and-down rectangular American log-face, his teeth shellacked. Was it normal? He'd been gone a month, only a month. Had he forgotten his own customs, the egg from which he'd hatched?

He took a stab at it in the next bathroom, realizing as he entered a stall that the bathrooms in Canada are designed for fat vulgar disgusting people. Same as the United States. In Korea the rooms are clean in the universities and subways and wherever you go. The commodes always are nice. You don't have to worry about dried slime on the seats, or nasty floors, piss everywhere, stupid graffiti to have to read. Here and there an *ajumma* enters while men urinate, to scrub out the commodes or wipe down the mirrors. Everything is designed with grace and an attention to function. The sinks are deep, wide so that the floors remain dry, and metal arms upon which spin large egg-shaped bars of marbled soap protrude from the counters. Soap! None of that idiotic squirt-your-soapy-foam-out-stuff going on. Nor do you see dispensers for toilet-seat shaped tissues meant for protecting one's derrière when it lands on a seat where other bare-bottomed men have sat. He was looking at one of those dispensers now, plastered to the wall, the portal to the Western World. He pulled one out and ripped it in such a way as that he could use it cleanly. Americans no doubt don't rip the fronts off the things, the result being that a little bit of piss gets on the edges, and on their clothes.

Americans don't use water (or their own saliva, such as did he) when they wipe. It's disturbing.

He did his business then got out of there. Browsed the duty-free shop. Purchased a large bottle of Canadian Club whiskey. The cashier wrapped it in a padded fishnet dress. From the duty-free shop he rolled along the thruway, fell into Starbucks. Tall coffee. Took it to a bathroom, spiked it. Found a seat not far from his gate. A smidgeon of privacy here, but filth all over, crumbs on the floor, coffee stains, juice stains, wrappers from chips and candies. A BO smell in the airport seats. He got up, found another seat nearby, but still the BO smell. Nothing for it. He drank the coffee, his back to the human flow.

They kept talking! Their voices emerged from nowhere. So many gross inflections. The horrid sounds, their inglorious arrivals announced by flipflops flapping happily, here came another gross mama farting through her nose for no good reason, grunting, coughing, groaning. They laughed. They snorted. They chortled.

A tall couple with a happily retarded adult son wearing a baseball cap walked by.

And wrinkly they were, repulsive, decaying, flakey, frizzled, fake and the women old and burned-out looking whatever their age.

The retarded son seemed all right. A smiler.

Hours Passed. At one point he nearly slept, but such near-sleep was lost through the shriek of a brat followed by the unpleasant voice of its mom: "We'll go see Mickey Mouse next year, honey." Behind his seat an airport exhibit of Disney characters, Goofys on pedestals and vintage Mickey Mouse watches behind glass, drew the brats. Whoever would've thought people would stop to look at that stuff? So much for the snooze. More shrieks. Only right over there, he realized, an airport playground for kids said *Come here turd munchers!* The stupid boys and stupid girls in stupid clothes—no fault of their own—flew shriekingly down plastic slides colored pink and blue, the fat mothers smiling over how cute they found it.

Even the kids, the little girls in short shorts, sported fields of cellulite on their thighs, their future shapes painfully evident.

Ugggh! He boarded the plane to LaGuardia. He arrived at LaGuardia and made it home to his rented room in Greenpoint, where he drank from the bottle of duty-free Canadian Club whiskey. Morning came. Time passed. He slept. He woke. He stretched. He yawned. His organs felt coated in slimy heavy rubber. His limbs. He bought half a gallon of Friendly's Cookie's N' Cream. Ate the whole thing while watching a stupid American movie in his room, the air-conditioner going. When catching glimpses of his face in the mirror, eating the ice-cream, he saw sadness. Pathetic. Pictured himself walking into the Polish hardware store for a length of rope.

He tried pulling himself together, getting into the spirit of New York. Wasn't New York the greatest city in the world? Many people would give an eyeball to live in Brooklyn, or pinky finger at the very least. *It's great,* he told himself, and went walking but they kept talking. "Don't touch those flowers, stupid," a Hispanic woman said to her child. Upon a garbage can somebody had written FUCK THIS WORLD. A short dumpy Mexican, pointing her cup of coffee at a jewelry store across the street, said to her short fat dumpy elderly companion, her father probably, "Mira. Y que es esso alli?"

To get away from the voices, and thinking he would admire the cityscape, he stepped down to Transmitter Park at the end of Greenpoint Avenue. He sat on a bench overlooking the East River and the awesome tall buildings beyond. He liked the Empire State Building and IBM building, pointed up top as they were. He breathed the sunshine in through his nose and let it out slow and closed his eyes and was beginning to feel relaxed, but a woman, fat as expected, flabby and wrinkly of arm even though she wasn't all that old, and pushing a baby buggy, sat down on the adjacent bench. The woman started talking on the phone to somebody. The woman had the New York accent. When the woman said, "my daughter"—my *daaa*tah—into the phone, it sounded like vomit coming out of her mouth. He tried to ignore it, tried to prove that he was not incapable of being around Americans, not so snobbish, not so antisocial, but she said, "my *daaa*tah" again. When she said it the third time, vomit jumped out of his mouth and splashed on the sidewalk in front of the bench, yellowish-brown in color, with bits of undigested lettuce, for he'd eaten a falafel sandwich not all that long ago. Some of the vomit got on his shirt. He felt feverish.

"Yellow Fever" is an infectious tropical disease carried by mosquitoes. Black vomit, he knew, was a symptom of yellow fever, but *his* vomit was brown. Good thing. He'd heard all the theories on why white guys, those devils, became obsessed with Asian women. They were gay. They were perverts. They were masochists. They wanted to be defiled. The theories were offensive, though he'd come across enough of the dudes with so-called Yellow Fever to know that a lot of it was true. Sadistic tendencies lurked below the surface, and he couldn't stand their company. He stopped going to the Meetup groups that put Asian women and white dudes, those devils, in the same room.

His mouth all vomity he rushed home to his room. Held his face in his pillow and sobbed. He was born. In the wrong. Body. In the wrong. Country. His heart was Korean. He was a Korean trapped in a tall white devil's body. Why was God mean to him? Why was he incapable of a broader perspective? Why so selfish? Didn't he know that he was worthless and didn't matter? Why did he want anything? It didn't make sense, yet he *wanted* desperately all the time.

He fell. Into a heavy depressed sleep. Whenever he woke a little and tried to rise up, to put on a face of *I can do it*, the feeling of a hopeless existence returned—with a heavy hand it pressed him into the sheets. "You gotta shake this shit!" he told himself, and left the apartment into the gross world, unlocked his bike downstairs. Got on it and rode by so many gross people—*fucking Americans!*—and again vomited, so rode back to his room and sobbed into his pillow.

WHITE ROSES

IN THE LIGHT by the water a woman played cello while a child in white did flute. Their notes carried over the pond, interrupted once by a train gliding by on its way to Manhattan. Within the music made by woman and child, women with long black hair came around. The women came amongst the people, passing out white roses.

In a lawn-chair up from the water sat a guy whose girlfriend was on the roster of people scheduled to speak. His girlfriend had not invited him to come, but he came. He wanted to add his number to the force against this evil at hand. He wanted to be of service to the women with long black hair.

A young dude with curly hair and fancy running sneakers got a rose. An old lady with snow white hair got a rose. People all around him were getting roses, so he wiggled in his chair, slightly agitated, as if saying *Over here, here I am, I'd love to get one too.*

The young women with long black hair passed him by, giving white roses to one and all, save him. They had armfuls, plenty to spare. Maybe they knew about him. Something told them. They felt it. They knew he was from a hot land, that he'd heard and repeated jokes as a child, and had stood around, as an adult, while friends went on about people who worked longer hours for less money, scooping up work that should have been theirs. Back then he was what people called a "redneck," and maybe a mere glance his way told them that that's what he once was, if he wasn't that still. Maybe the women with long black hair knew that his girlfriend was embarrassed by him, or that he'd seen their bodies stripped bare and brutalized online. Those *fantasy* videos were only a hop, skip, and jump from the true-life scenarios where mothers and grandmothers were dropped to the sidewalks these days of the "kung flu."

The song of the cello and flute ended and those gathered around the duck pond clapped. A female professor then said some things into the microphone and people clapped. A councilwoman too said some things, raising her fist as a new train pounded by. Two youngsters from the township high school, a boy and girl, went up and spoke, first the girl, a regular middle-class white person, and then the boy, who read his essay about how messed up things became once the coronavirus hit, how so many of his privileges were stripped away. People saw him different now. No longer could he waltz into Starbucks of a summer's day sweating with no shirt on. The support coming in from the larger community and throughout the neighborhoods was appreciated, he said, but much of it, he knew, was for show, done out of political necessity. He finished his essay to strong, heartfelt applause, and the guy in the lawn-chair thought: *This could be the future president.*

The mayor stepped up to the lectern, this mayor who resembled Senator Cory Booker from nearby Newark. He was bald and black and a similar rhythm and ethos came out in his words. After his speech, the mayor mentioned that his childhood friend had flown in from Chicago to be here tonight. The friend, who was Asian, went up to the lectern and the two men embraced for all to see. Another train passed along the tracks above the duck pond. Another woman with long black hair streaming down her back sang opera, forehead crinkled with yearning, and a sadness dedicated to the women whose faces were displayed on the poster attached to the lectern—those women.

The guy's girlfriend, the poet, was introduced by a woman who looked very proud to be introducing her. The woman looked smitten as she read out his girlfriend's accomplishments, the magazines she had published in, and the awards she had won. At the end of her introduction, the introducer didn't want to move away from the lectern. She wanted to stay there, in solidarity, so in solidarity stood. As his girlfriend read a poem, looking fierce and limitless, the woman who'd introduced her beamed, all this admiration as gusts of wind tossed around their long black hair. *I love my girlfriend*, the guy in the lawn-chair thought. After the poem, his girlfriend spoke some words about women warriors.

It was dark now, and the final woman at the lectern, another woman with long black hair, said, "We gave to everybody here white roses. We passed them out to you at the beginning. The roses represent our commitment. The white roses are a symbol, a token, a statement that we are going to try harder to release this hatred, to make a renewed commitment to fight."

The guy, from his lawn-chair, looked around.

He had not been invited, but had come.

"Let us now release our white roses into the pond," the beautiful woman with long black hair said, and the guy watched the mixed families and old ladies and the young dude with curly hair and fancy running sneakers—they all stepped down to the water of the duck pond, and surrounded the small pond as if to embrace it as a community. They released their roses into the water, pushing them out like paper boats.

Then the people, many shivering from the cold that had set in deep as night began, hurried away from the water, moving away from the pond in the direction of the street where their cars and utility vehicles were parked. The guy remained in his chair, eyes fixed on the pond whose roses shimmered in the moonlight, a small galaxy of flowering matter. He looked for his girlfriend and saw her on the other side of the water. They locked eyes and right then a cloud cut below the moon and the twinkling stars dimmed.

THE SLUG

YOUR MOTHER was fond of me.

I never told you, but one day, when I came over, she opened the door but did not invite me in. Your mother stood there looking at me getting rained on. I wore a fedora hat and the drops tapped it. I think she liked the way I looked in the rain. I think she thought it was nice, me in the rain in my hat.

She invited me in. In the kitchen she made lemon tea and we drank it at the table, chatting while you upstairs watched *Star Trek*, the one where the monster goes around raping pretty girls and.

I remember your face at my place south of town, your "little man's" body naked on my bed, that face with eyes flashing bright and angry. What do you want? you kept saying, clutching my face with both your hands.

Your sizable mother asked did I have a cold. She said I was nasal. I'm fine, I said, but she said no, you gotta try this, and opened the back door where it still was raining.

I want to give you the slug, she said. The slug? I said, and she showed me that cleansing thing you hippies do, where you stuff the spout of that watering-can-thing in your nose and dump its contents down your nasal passage so that it comes out in the back of your throat. With all that rain coming down onto my face I choked on it, coughing. Everything about it felt backwards. I spit it out onto the muddy ground where the slug foamed up white on brown. I felt as if I'd been in the ocean, my face having been dragged along the bottom.

What do you want? you said, and.

I said, I want to *fffff*.

You thought I was Christly when all I was was weird, a little weak-hearted maybe; but it was fun, acting out our lives in our magical wood. I baptized you in the green "watah," holding you under too long. I could have drowned you that fall, my friend, but instead I pulled you up, your little man's head coughing, wet, and carried you to the shore. I felt heroic that day, grand, as if I'd saved your beautiful self, your precious life so wonderful and crazy, so supple, so totally lovely.

Say it, you said.

I want to fuck you, I said, and after that it came easy, those words that at first were hard to say and.

What are you doing? you said and.

I said, I'm fucking you.

What? you said.

I set you in the leaves, your slender bronze body breaking them. If leaves could think, those leaves would have thought they were lucky to hold you, to be broken by you, but I am not a leaf.

Why on earth did you tell your mother?

I know you told her. After the slug that day, when my head was wet, and my fingers dripped, and everything in the world was off and backwards, she wanted to know if you "peaked." I had no idea, at first, what she was after, but the bits of sound falling from her lips gathered into a crystal globe.

Still, I played dumb, and your mom dropped the ambiguities. When you fuck her, does she orgasm?

While upstairs you watched *Star Trek*, the one where the monster goes around raping pretty girls.

Your mother, seeing me all nervous, all distressed, put her hand on my forearm, as if for support. I wanted to yank it away, but I said, I love your firstborn.

Your mother pursed her lips, shaking her head, looking off into space. Was your mother flirting? Was she exhibiting signs of jealousy? Was she trying to give permission where permission wasn't hers to give?

I can't say, but she kept at it until I told her you did.

Your mother smiled and.

I climbed the stairs and found you stomach-down on your mother's bed, watching *Star Trek*. You said, This is so sick. There's a monster going around raping people.

People? I said.

Girls, you said.

Really? I said.

Does that make you excited? you said.

No, what on earth are you saying?

Remember when you told me that your last girlfriend would come home and rape you?

Yes.

I just want you to know that rape is when somebody has sex with you against your will.

I was dumb, it's true. What did I know of girls and monsters and.

Rape and.

I loved you eating, so much, you sitting on my rug and pulling nervously at the shag, being you. Our first time alone in a dusky room. I could sit in front of you for hours, just looking at you, just staring into your eyes for hours, into your bronze face, or at your lovely feet, one of which you drew for me, pastels on rag paper, and signed with a red heart of love. "The Divine Worm," you titled the drawing. I prize it, but don't hang it up. I'm worried it could make your mother jealous.

Your musical yawns, I loved them.

Your underarms, I sucked on them.

It was your mother who told me. I helped her, comforted her. We did that for each other. And at the party, when the others weren't looking, I was busy licking you off my fingers. There was even a bone, and I held it between my jaw and cheek—a piece of your arm, I imagined—and swallowed it.

What are you doing? you whispered.

Ffffff.

I was dead. Empty. A never-ending sliver of agony. You were gone, but your mother's mouth was not so unlike yours. We cried on each other's shoulders, and when the guests left went upstairs. You need healing, your mother said, so I laid on the bed, same bed you watched *Star Trek* from that day of the slug, on your stomach, divine worms in the air behind you, ankles knocking playfully.

In the light pouring through the windows she took off my clothes and practiced Quantum-Touch Therapy on me, and the techniques of an obscure spirituality, and she spanked me. I felt as if I was being punished, but she turned me onto my back. I didn't resist. It was even lovely at first, but your mother is on the large side. It may have been comic, what we did, but what choice did we have? We were all we had left of you, and no, she did not hold my face in both hands and stare with yearning passion into my eyes. What do you want? she did not say, nor What are you doing? She merely smeared me over the sheets, and I melted, sinking stinkingly into the awful drowning grief as you, my dear precious gummy little man, waved goodbye.

SPRUCE TIPS

THE FATHER on the porch does things with a knife to a fish. The mother in the kitchen, cradling the baby, watches the father through the glass window. The father smiles at the mother and the baby, one of his front teeth fake and discolored. He's large, the father, with a big long head. He is handsome with his knife, and what a sweet manly voice he has! His caring voice says "I love you," over and over to the girl baby as he puts her to sleep nights. Mornings, he pats around the house drinking coffee from a mug. He'll sit in the living room rocker, the genitals under the black flaps of terrycloth robe in the shadows, a heap of silent something in a mountain recess where sleeping bears wait for spring, or brain.

Your baby's brain must be treated with great care, experts tell them.

They are their own experts, not for the subscription to *Mothers and Babies* that tells of brain food diets, how cloth diapers are the way to go, but for the love they hold for the girl baby. The love they hold will protect her brain. The mother plays banjo for the baby, plays guitar soft for soft ears.

The mother is a fine musician, a snowboarder, but there will be no ice or powder for the mother now.

Even if she, the mother, cared to head up the mountain to ride fast, the month is wrong. It is late May, spring in blossom, the mountains shifting in and out of God's light. A half a rainbow out there is lodged into a colorful mist upon the water. The mother has taken the baby to the living room and, from the blanket by the great floor-to-ceiling windows, her white-whiskered black dog standing by, doggy sentry, she says, "Look, see that? It's a rainbow. It means God has promised not to drown us again."

She was better off alone, some experts say, and speak of how, oh, when they have a baby there is no way in the world they will take painkillers. It means you don't love your baby if you take painkillers. They say if you love your baby, what grows inside your body, not only will you embrace the pain that comes from being pregnant, from giving birth, but hope for more, more pain—the more you suffer, they say, the stronger your love.

Twisted people. What do they know of motherhood and babies?

Have you talked to a baby? What do you say to a baby?

The father bounces the baby. He says, "You live in the lap of luxury. Will you buy it?"

A grand specimen of a dad! A grand husband! See the daddy whisk the girl baby away to the player piano. He sits on the bench, the girl baby in his lap, and pumps the pedals with his large bare feet. The keys dance below her eyes, playing *The Sound of Music*. They have been told by experts—everybody is an expert when it comes to babies—that the baby, when she transmogrifies into a child, will not remember this, the keys, will not remember the father's expert hands. Other experts say the sounds from the piano cut grooves into their girl baby's brain. Be careful about what grooves you cut into your little baby's brain.

The mother holds the baby high. She says, "Sweet baby."

One expert says when you bounce a baby, a groove is cut into her brain.

The father is finished with his fish. The fish he takes inside and slips a slice of it into the frying pan to fry. It is a nice house they live in, a great beautiful nice house owned by the mother's father. The great floor-to-ceiling windows were imported from Seattle. And the kitchen is full of spices and stainless utensils. The fish in the pan hisses in the oil, in the garlic steam.

But you hear things. Once fall the mother was busted up, her bruises emerald. The father was her boyfriend then. There were drugs. He drank. That's what the experts say. That was before they married, when the mother, escaping the would-be hunk of a daddy, spent the winter in a tent on a hill. Everybody thought her such a hero, just ask the experts. She built her own fires and showered once a week at the high school gym.

The father pokes the fish with a fork.

And the mother nurses the baby.

The experts have driven up the mountain. In the yard they pick baby spruce tips to make beer with. As the mother nurses the girl baby, she watches her friends through the large windows, and wants, just look at her forehead, crinkled and wanting, to go out there, do that, pick baby spruce tips.

The mother and her baby.

Some experts, talking behind their backs, marvel over the lives of them, the luxury of them.

And the mother looks awful great. Take off her shoes, you'll see. Take off her socks. Her feet alone prove she is a great mother. See her play banjo, sit, or pull out her tit. We love when she does that. The baby sucks it, her throat in motion as the mother looks out the window. Her body was made to save the world, we say, or the whales that wait for fall in Berners Bay, sucking down schools of wiggling fish. The fish will help the whales in their swim to the warmer waters of Hawaii. The mother is from Kentucky. She stands, brushes her hair. The bruises on her face never quite healed, and one expert says that the mother is not bright. Look at her face, the expert says, and we look. The mother's face looks like an aerial photo of the Inside Passage in winter, a blur of white through which, here and there, an island can be seen.

BOLD

For those who dare, anything is possible.
— The Monk

MY DAD DIED in June and my wife left me in July. I tell you upfront so that if a self-pitying note creeps into my voice, you won't ditch this before it gets going. She did it behind my back, at first. She would have continued in that vein had I not discovered his name on her cell phone, a long list of Seths under her received and outgoing calls. It was while we were visiting my hometown in Florida during my summer break from school. I was a year shy of an MFA in poetry.

Now it is late August. During my mental breakdown, an old friend lent me her shoulder to cry on. This friend had connections in the world of wildlife workers, and was friends with a Ranger who knew of a job opening that didn't pay much, but would give me a place to get my head straight and recover from the ordeal. I withdrew from the university, and moved into a Jetstream at the trailhead of the Apalachicola National Forest, not but ten miles from where my wife now lived with this guy she reconnected with on Facebook.

My job is simple: be here throughout the day, sleep here, keep an eye on things, don't let happen what happened seven years ago, how some teens came in and lit a bonfire that burned out of control and basically made desolate a large portion of the park area.

It's boring, but in the mornings I run. I run and run and keep on running through the sand, barefoot the way I like to run. I run down narrow trails leading through scrub oak and up hills, dip down into dry sinkholes, and I run until I can run no more, which is about six miles, a big circle that I finish off by tripping over a log at Big Dismal sink, one of the park's main attractions. I trip over the log and fall over thirty feet and hit the cold black water. It's always a real wakeup call, and the fine thing about it is that I never know if when I hit I'm going to slam into the big log that has been floating around on the surface of the sink like a speck in somebody's eye for as long as any of the rangers can remember. There's always the chance that I will become paralyzed or die, and that is comforting. I float around in the water a bit, then scale the clay walls and walk back to the Jetstream and start a pot of coffee. Sometimes I try to write a poem or two, but can't. All I do is brood. And besides, poetry is stupid.

ACKNOWLEDGEMENTS

Stories from this collection have appeared in the following journals: "Gary Gets Gary" and "Spruce Tips" in *Juked*; "Alive in the Jungle" in *The Dead Mule School of Southern Literature*; "Intensive" in *Heavy Glow*; "Bumpy" in *Meat for Tea*; "Pollen" in *Bull*; "Cozy" in *Raleigh Review*; "Ajax" in *Third Wednesday*; "The Slug" in *Existere*; "Dorm" in *The Writing Disorder*; "What Henry Needs" and "Scarecrow" in *Dogzplot*; "Forty" in *Medulla Review*; "How We Solved the Problem" in *Treehouse*; "Possum" in *Grey Sparrow Review*; "Dandruff" in *New Stone Circle*; "Noodles and Socks" in *The Boiler*; "Dude" in *Toad*; "Bold" in *Monkeybicycle*; "Pam" in *Knee-Jerk Magazine*; "Christmas in Queens" in *Mr. Beller's Neighborhood*; "Faulkner at 110" in *Red Fez*; "These Kids Were the Chosen Ones" in *The Delinquent*; "Black Vomit" in *Black Scat Review*; "Horse's Dad, Uhm" in *Thin Air Magazine*; "Boulders" in *BODY*. Photos are by the author.

THE AUTHOR

John Oliver Hodges was born in Tallahassee. His published books include *Quizzleboon* (a novel), *The Love Box* (short stories) and *Eating My Name* (a memoir on Kindle). As a teenager he was guitarist for the American hardcore band, Hated Youth.